INEVITABLE DISCOVERY

BY USA TODAY BESTSELLING AUTHOR

MELISSA F. MILLER

BROWN STREET BOOKS

eBook ISBN 978-1-940759-54-8

"Never, ever be afraid to make some noise and get in good trouble, necessary trouble."
Representative John Lewis
(1940-2020)

"Fight for the things that you care about, but do it in a way that will lead others to join you."
Justice Ruth Bader Ginsburg
(1933-2020)

"Give sorrow words. The grief that does not speak whispers the o'er-fraught heart, and bids it break."
William Shakespeare,
Macbeth, Act IV, Scene 3, ll. 209-10

1

Saturday, November 20, 1999
5:40 A.M.
Georgetown University Campus
Washington, D.C.

The shrill ring of the telephone was muffled, but not muffled enough. On the top bunk, Sasha rolled onto her stomach and pressed her pillow down over her head to wait for the ringing to stop.

The ringing continued.

"Sasha, phone," Allie moaned from the lower bunk.

Sasha ignored the phone and her roommate.

The ringing continued, as did the groaning from the bottom bunk.

"Please. I feel sick."

Sasha bit back the words that rushed to her lips and pushed off her comforter, untangling it from her feet.

Of course, Allie felt sick. She'd probably spent most of the night drinking grain alcohol punch at some friend of a friend's house party. At least, Sasha assumed so. She hadn't shown up at the library for their Friday cram session. So Sasha had sat alone in the carrel they'd reserved, rereading her notes on Beowulf for the eighth time and pretending not to notice the library emptying out as the sun set and the weekend started.

She stumbled down the ladder and walked blindly toward the cordless phone's base. Empty. As usual. She turned in a slow circle, searching for the source of the high-pitched ring. After a moment, she pinpointed the sound and yanked the handset out from under Allie's quilted jacket.

"Why is your jacket on the floor?"

"Why is the phone on the floor?" Allie shot back, before flinging her arm over her eyes and rolling toward the wall.

Sasha fumbled with the button. "Hello?"

"Sasha, were you sleeping?"

She squinted at the alarm clock. "Mom, it's not even six o'clock in the morning. What do you think?"

"I'm sorry, honey." Her mother's voice cracked on the words, and Sasha's irritation turned to worry.

Valentina McCandless never apologized.

"Is something wrong?" Her heart clenched. "Is it Nana?"

In the periphery of her vision, she saw Allie roll slowly toward her and stare out at her with wide, blue eyes.

"No. It's ... your brother."

Before Sasha could ask *which* brother, her mom broke into loud, wordless sobbing.

"Mom? Mom?"

Her mother's cries faded and her dad's voice sounded in her ear. "Hi, kiddo." He sounded tired. No, more than tired. Drained, lifeless.

"Dad? What's going on? Who's in trouble? Wait, let me guess—Ryan."

"Patrick's dead."

Dead? Patrick?

He couldn't be. Her heart roared in her ears

and she gripped the phone as if it was keeping her upright. Maybe it was.

After a million years, she choked out a jumble of words. "I don't ... no. No. Patrick's not *dead*! What are you talking about?"

She felt rather than saw Allie bolt up from the bed and race across the room to hover behind her.

"He is, honey."

The heaviness in the words landed on her, and she curved herself forward, bending and wrapping her free hand around her waist. Allie rubbed her back while she gulped for air.

"What happened—a car accident?" She finally managed to ask.

A long pause. She heard his breath hitch.

"Dad?"

"He was shot, Sasha."

"Shot?" She echoed numbly.

"The Atlantic City police called. All we know now is that he was dead on the scene. Mom and I have to leave. We're driving up there to ... to claim his body."

Nothing he said made sense. For a moment, it was a relief. Maybe Patrick wasn't dead. Maybe her dad had suffered a stroke. Why would

Patrick be in New Jersey? She straightened and turned around to flash Allie a weak *'I'm okay'* smile. Allie studied her with grave eyes.

Then she remembered. Patrick and his buddies had gone to AC for a guys' weekend to celebrate his thirtieth birthday. Her heart hit her stomach with a lurch.

"Dad, you know Patrick's friends. Maybe this is a really sick joke?" She reached for the idea, ridiculous as it was.

"It's not a joke. I just pray to the Lord that Sean is okay."

"Sean was with him?"

"Yeah, he tagged along. Ry had to work. So he can pick you up at the train station when you get in. If you call the house and he's not there, call Nana. You'll probably get home before we do."

Logistical concerns started to break through the frozen cloud of disbelief and pain that covered her brain. She already had a ticket home for Thanksgiving break, but it was for Tuesday. Could she change it? Would there be a fee?

She had money on her cafeteria card, but, unfortunately, Amtrak didn't take Georgetown dining plan credits. Her next work study check wouldn't come until the end of next week. She glanced at Allie. She hated to ask, but she might have to.

"Okay, Dad. I love you."

"I love you, too, pumpkin. Be careful, okay? I have to go. Mom's waiting in the car."

The line clicked off. She stared down at the phone, suddenly unable to remember what to do with it.

Allie seemed to understand her problem and gently pried the handset out of Sasha's clenched hand. She powered it off and returned it to the base to charge. Then she turned and searched Sasha's face. "Your brother's dead?"

Sasha blinked and nodded.

Allie wrapped her in a hug. Sasha fought back her tears and focused on the smell of Allie's pear glacé body lotion. The familiar sweet scent was a lifeline.

"What can I do to help?"

"I need to change my train ticket. And pack. And I guess let the TAs know. And ..."

Allie cut her off. "One thing at a time. Start with the ticket."

"Do you know if there's a change fee?"

Allie shrugged. Right. She didn't queue up at Union Station like the rest of them. She flew back and forth from school on her dad's private jet. Why would she know?

"Don't worry about that." She rifled through her desk drawer and pulled out a fistful of twenties. Sasha opened her mouth to object, but Allie was already pushing the money into her hand. "I get my allowance next week. Forget the train. Fly."

"I'll pay you back."

"I know."

"Allie—"

"Look, don't thank me. I'm sure my dad made that money evicting widows and orphans or draining pensioners' retirement accounts. Just get home to your family." Her eyes brightened. "I know, I'll come with you. You shouldn't be alone."

Sure, Allie loved the loud, ragtag McCandless clan. She'd stayed with them for almost a month last summer while her parents were in Europe. But, seriously, she'd pass up Thanksgiving in Malibu to go to a funeral in Pittsburgh?

"You're kidding, right?"

In response, she opened their shared closet and tugged her titanium suitcase and Sasha's black duffel bag down from the top shelf. Allie's kindness breached the dam, and the tears Sasha'd been holding at bay spilled over.

"Thank you." She smiled at her friend through wet eyes. She really didn't want to have to do this alone. Thank God for Allie.

She sank to her knees on the rough carpet and buried her face in her hands.

Patrick was dead.

2

Wednesday, November 20, 2019
3:27 A.M.
Pittsburgh, Pennsylvania

The metallic chirp of the cell phone jolted Sasha from sleep. She bolted upright, breathing hard. Beside her, Connelly stirred. She fumbled for the phone while her heart drummed fast against the thin fabric of her tank top.

She grabbed it and answered without checking the caller ID on the display. "Sasha McCandless."

"I'm so sorry to bother you so late ... I didn't know who else to call."

Jordana Morgan's voice was nearly unrecognizable—higher pitched and faster than usual, and dripping with urgency and fear.

"It's okay," she soothed her legal intern in a whisper.

She glanced at Connelly, who'd thrown an arm over his eyes. That wasn't going to block out the conversation. She eased herself out of bed and headed for the walk-in closet. With any luck, from inside the closet, her voice wouldn't carry across the hall and wake the twins. Or the pets.

She closed the door behind her with a soft click and sank cross-legged into a pile of dry cleaning.

"What's going on?"

She expected to hear that the girl had locked herself out of her apartment or run out of gas or even had trusted the wrong designated driver and needed a ride back to campus. She absolutely did not anticipate what she heard.

"I'm at the police station."

"What?"

"I've been arrested. I mean, I guess? I got

picked up at the protest ... Sasha, I can't make bail."

"Wait. Stop. Have you been Mirandized?"

"Um, no? I don't know." Her voice rose in a wail, and Sasha could hear the tears right behind it, threatening to spill out.

Did this kid not watch TV? "Has someone in a uniform read you your Miranda rights?"

"No."

"Good. Which station? Five?"

"No, I'm not in the city."

"Where are you then?"

She heard muffled voices.

Jordana came back on the line. "The officer says I'm in Milltown at the station on Steel Avenue."

"Okay. Don't talk to the officer again. Do you understand?"

"Yeah, but she's really ni—"

"Do *not* talk to her."

Jordana fell silent.

"Don't talk to anybody until I get there. Just hold tight. I'll be there as fast as I can."

"Thank you, Sasha. I couldn't call my mom. She'd freak."

"Don't worry about it." She reached for a pair

of sweats and reconsidered. She trapped the phone between her ear and her neck and pulled a tailored dress from the nearest hanger.

As she was wiggling into it, Jordana started yammering.

"I can't believe this is happening to me. We were just peacefully protesting. We marched from campus to the overpass where they shot Vaughn Tabor. I guess that's outside the city limits, but we weren't being disruptive. It was a silent vigil. And then the cops—"

"Jordana! Quiet!" She used the tone the dog trainer had finally convinced her to take with Mocha to get her to stop barking. *Remember, you're not asking her, you're telling her.*

It had mixed results with the dog, but it seemed to work like a charm with the girl.

"Sorry," Jordana said meekly.

"It's okay. You can tell me all about it in the car. But, please, just zip it until I get there."

"It's zipped."

"Good."

She ended the call and was struggling with her own zipper when the closet door opened to reveal Connelly. He smiled sleepily at her from beneath a mop of sleep-mussed hair.

"Need a hand?"

"Please."

She turned. He zipped up her dress, then handed her the matching suit coat. "Do I want to know?"

She belted the long jacket and jammed her feet into a pair of high-heeled boots. "Jordana's been arrested."

He blinked. "I'll start the coffee while you brush your teeth and hair."

"Man, I love you."

"I know it."

She reached up and ruffled his hair. "You need a haircut."

He grabbed her hand and kissed her fingers. "Who's Allie?"

She froze. "What?"

"You were talking in your sleep. You kept saying '*Allie, Allie.*'"

She pulled her hand away and smoothed her jacket. "Um, Allie Peterman was my roommate my freshman and sophomore years."

"What happened?" He frowned at her. "I've never heard you mention her. She wasn't at the wedding, was she?"

"No." She sidled past him and headed into

the bathroom. He trailed her, unwilling to drop the topic.

She searched the vanity for her glasses and answered without looking at him. "She didn't come back to school after the winter break. We lost touch."

She could feel him watching her as she ran a brush through her tangle of hair.

"You were close."

It wasn't a question. She answered it anyway. "I thought we were, but I guess I was wrong. She ghosted me. I called her parents' place a bunch of times, but ... I never heard back from her."

"I'm sorry."

She shrugged off his gentle invitation to talk about it and met his eyes. "That coffee's not going to make itself."

He quirked his mouth but didn't shift his gaze. "Message delivered. Allie from college is off-limits." He dropped a kiss on the crown of her head. "You should wear your glasses more often. They make you look formidable."

"I can work with that." She flashed him a smile as he edged through the doorway.

She tried to remember her dream while she brushed her teeth, but it was gone, evaporated, chased away by the insistent ringing of the phone.

She glanced down at the phone on the vanity to check the time and nearly swallowed a mouthful of minty toothpaste when she noted the date. November 20. Exactly twenty years since the early morning phone call that had turned her world upside down.

She gave herself a fierce look in the mirror. "Think about Patrick later. Right now, you need to help Jordana." She said the words formidably —she hoped.

SASHA'S HEADLIGHTS washed over the concrete block police station, lighting it up in the darkness, as she pulled into the closest available parking space. She sat in the warm car for a moment, enjoying the heat and savoring the last mouthful of coffee in her travel mug.

Then she squared her shoulders, swiped her lips with the brownish-red lipstick that Naya promised suited her, and killed the engine. She dropped the lipstick tube into the center console and checked her handiwork in the visor mirror.

Game time.

She hurried out of the car and across the parking lot, steeling herself against the cold wind. Just in case anyone was watching from the lobby, she swung her briefcase in time with the crisp click of her heeled boots against the pavement as she marched toward the entrance. The bag was empty save for a legal pad, a pen, her wallet, and her cell phone, but only a fool rode into battle without her armor.

She pulled open the heavy door and stepped inside, grateful for the blast of hot air that hit her in the face. A quick scan of the lobby revealed that her theatrics had been for an audience of no one. The wooden counter that anchored the space was unattended. A blinking computer monitor and the staticky buzz of a police radio were the only signs of life.

She searched the desk for a bell to ring or a button to push to announce her arrival but saw nothing. She craned her neck in both directions. The halls were dimly lit and silent.

Patience was never her strong suit—a fact that was doubly true before sunrise. She waited another thirty seconds, then darted behind the desk and through the open door set in the wall.

The smell of coffee led her to a cramped kitchenette with a refrigerator, a small stove and microwave, and a wood laminate table shoved up against one wall. A tall red-haired guy who looked as tired as she felt was pouring coffee from a glass pot into a "World's Best Dad" mug.

She knocked on the doorframe. "Hi."

He raised an eyebrow. "You're not supposed to be back here."

"Sorry," she said in a voice that didn't carry so much as a hint of apology. "There's nobody out front. I really need to spring my client and get back home before my twins wake up." She nodded at the mug in his hand. "You know how it is."

He gave her a quizzical look, then glanced down at the lettering on his mug. "Oh. Nope. Can't say that I do. This is just some random mug from the cabinet."

Crap.

"Oh. Regardless, my legal intern was picked up at the protest earlier. I need to speak to the arresting officer."

The guy rubbed his temple. "We have a busload of protestors. And two officers total to process them. Your intern probably hasn't been charged with anything. It's just taking some time to get through everyone."

"You can't detain citizens indefinitely without charging them. You know that right?" She eyed him coldly.

He raised the coffee to his lips and took a sip, then grimaced. "Ugh. Burnt. So, you a lawyer?"

"I am." She twitched her lips. The attempt to connect parent-to-parent had failed, but maybe she could reach him through an actual shared interest. "A dash of cinnamon—or, even better, cardamon, if you have it—will help with the burnt taste."

He showed the first signs of life. "Oh, yeah?"

"Yep."

He rummaged in the cabinet over the microwave and dug out a jar of cinnamon. He shook it over the mug and stirred it into his coffee. She waited while he took another appraising sip.

"Not bad." He nodded. "So, this client of yours, what's her name? Maybe I can light a fire under Officer Diamond."

She gave him her warmest smile. "I'd appreciate anything you could do. Her name is Jordana

Morgan. But how do you know which of the two officers is processing her?"

"Diamond took the females. Officer Willard is handling the males. Follow me," he waved a hand and headed toward the door as he explained.

"So, how many protestors did you say they picked up?"

"More than thirty. They were blocking the travel lane. Right around a blind corner, after dark. Those dang kids are lucky nobody got hit by a car." He shook his head.

She smiled noncommittally. She unavoidably had to talk to these people to get Jordana out of here, but the less she said, the better.

Officer Not-A-Dad led her to a bland conference room and told her to take a seat. She scrolled through her phone answering emails until the door opened and a pale, silent Jordana walked into the room with a motherly looking police officer gripping her arm.

Sasha rushed around the table and gave Jordana a hug. Then she pulled back and studied her tear-streaked face. However bad her night had been, it was over now.

"You her mom?" Officer Diamond asked,

looking Sasha up and down. She took in the charcoal gray suit, the glasses, and the briefcase.

"No, I'm her lawyer. And her friend."

"Hmm. Well, she's free to go. You can pick up her personal effects at the front desk on your way out."

Jordana wilted. Whether from relief or exhaustion, Sasha couldn't tell.

"She hasn't been charged with anything?"

"Citation for impeding the flow of traffic."

Sasha turned to Jordana. "How long have you been here?"

"I dunno. I don't even know what time it is. It was before midnight when they picked us up. I know that."

"You've kept these college students here for hours in the middle of the night to issue *citations?*"

"Look, Ms ..."

"McCandless-Connelly."

Diamond set her mouth in a hard line. Her voice was weary. "Right. Look, we're a small PD. We're processing them as fast as we can. We're supposed to go in alphabetical order, but we bumped Ms. Morgan here to the front as a courtesy. But I'm on the 'F's, so if you want me to put her back in line, I'll be happy to."

Jordana tugged on Sasha's sleeve. "Please," she whimpered.

Sasha held the officer's eyes for a long moment before relenting. "Good night, Officer Diamond."

"Ms. McCandless-Connelly." The woman nodded, then shifted her gaze to Jordana. "And, you, missy, stay out of the roadway while you're exercising your First Amendment rights."

"Or you could stop shooting motorists and we won't need—"

Glad as Sasha was to see a spark of life in her intern, this was neither the time nor the place. She put a hand on the small of Jordana's back, whispered, "Zip it," in her ear, and piloted her past the police officer and out into the hall.

At the front desk, Jordana signed for her phone and student ID while Sasha asked her new friend for the name of the nearest open coffee shop.

As they exited the building, a stocky man on his way into the station held the door for them. Sasha noted his salt-and-pepper hair, expensive pinstripe suit, and cashmere scarf and gave him a friendly nod.

"Looks like at least one of your friends also has a lawyer on speed dial," she observed to Jordana.

The girl mumbled an indecipherable response as she trudged out into the cold night, shivering in a light jacket.

Sasha stifled her urge to comment on the importance of weather-appropriate clothing and put her arm around Jordana's shoulders. "Come on, I'll buy you a coffee."

3

L andon turned and watched the petite brunette in the ridiculous boots guide a purple-haired girl toward a gray station wagon.

He waited until the headlights flared to life, then turned away.

"Hiya, Paul."

"Mr. Lewis, sir." The officer behind the desk straightened his posture and raised a 'World's Best Dad' mug in salute. "Can I offer you a cup of coffee?"

"Your coffee sucks."

"That it does. But turns out if you sprinkle some cinnamon in it, it's drinkable."

"Cinnamon, eh? The sun's not even up yet and I've already learned something new today."

"You and me both. That lady lawyer told me." He jerked his chin toward the parking lot.

"One of the protesters called a lawyer? Huh. You catch a name?"

"Sorry, no."

Kara Diamond stuck her head through the doorway. "McCandless-Connelly. She said the girl works for her. The girl's name is Morgan— Jordana Morgan."

Landon stroked his chin and thought. "This bears watching."

"Sir?"

Paul tented his eyebrows, questioning.

"Talking to myself."

The lawyer and her employee did bear watching, but he'd handle it privately.

"Oh, okay. Right. Here's the list of protestors." Paul handed over a single sheet, still warm from the printer.

Landon flicked his gaze down the page, skimming the names. "All students at the university?"

"Yep."

"What about the information on the others?"

The police officer slid a sealed manila envelope across the countertop. Landon folded it lengthwise and tucked it into his chest pocket. "Great, thanks."

Kara jutted her chin toward his pocket. "Those guys, the ones who went to PPC, what did they do?"

He smiled. "Nothing. Yet."

The officers shot him a pair of confused frowns, but he didn't elaborate. It was true that he needed the cooperation of local law enforcement to run his beta tests, but the fewer details he shared with the testers, the better. The Predictive and Preventive Crime Program was continually being refined, tweaked, and improved. Until he had a program he was ready to go public with, there was no upside in talking about it.

"But—"

"Thanks for this." He tapped his chest and cut off the officer before she could press him.

As he turned to leave, a door at the far left end of the hallway swung open, and a short, balding officer ushered a tall, broad-shouldered teenager through the doorway. He loped more than walked, slouching, with his hands jammed into the pockets of his gray hooded sweatshirt.

Josh.

Landon's heart thumped against his ribcage and his throat closed.

A moment later, the kid glanced in his direction. His face was all wrong. The eyes were close-set, not wide. The lips were full, not thin. There was no dimple in his chin.

Not Josh.

Of course it was not Josh. His brain wasted no time berating him for the mistake. Josh has been dead for twelve years. If he *were* alive, he'd be a man in his thirties, not a scruffy college kid out protesting in the middle of the night. He'd probably have a job, a spouse, maybe even a child—

Landon shook his head to stop the train of thought before it ran him over and left him plastered all over the tracks.

The officer nodded as he escorted Not Josh to the front desk to gather his personal belongings. Landon swallowed hard and nodded back. He hurried out of the building and into the whipping wind on legs that trembled, shook, and threatened to give out completely.

He made it back to his sedan on autopilot and slid into the driver's seat. He gripped the leather-covered steering wheel, pressed his head back against the headrest, and squeezed his eyes shut.

Josh.

He'd lived with the loss of Josh for a dozen years and the enormity of the hole in his life had never, not for a moment, lessened. The death of his only child had cleaved his life into two: Before and After. And every good thing in the After—every holiday, every sunset, every accolade—was tinged with the pain of Josh not being there.

When Deanne finally left him, after all the counseling and the fighting and the trial separations, she'd told him she simply couldn't love two ghosts. But Landon couldn't find a way to let go —not of Josh, and not of the way he'd been ripped from their lives.

All that mattered, the *only* thing that mattered now, was that he devote his remaining days on the earth to his work. Deanne thought he was motivated by their loss, by his own grief. But it was more than that.

What he wanted, more than anything, was to spare even one other family from that midnight knock on the door. Spare them from seeing two grave-faced police officers on the doorstep. Spare them from hearing the words *"Your son's been shot. I'm sorry, sir. He didn't make it."* And spare them from the breathless spiral into endless darkness that would follow.

He sat in the car, eyes closed, hands clenched like claws around the steering wheel, for a long time until his breathing returned to normal and his nausea ebbed. Then he removed the sealed envelope from his breast pocket and slit it open with his fingernail.

He spread the sheet out flat over the steering wheel and studied the list of names, backgrounds, and arrest records. His mind whirred as he digested the information, calculated threat ratings, and churned out hypotheses and recommended outcomes.

The computer could do it faster. But he assessed risk more accurately than Cesare did. The artificial intelligence program was, in many ways, a child—learning, adapting, growing. In contrast, Landon had years of experience to draw upon. One day very soon, though, Cesare would be able to make the judgments more quickly and more accurately than Landon, or any police officer, psychologist, social worker, or judge could ever hope to. And that was the day Landon would finally be able to honor Josh's memory, to say his murder hadn't been for nothing.

He shoved the list back into the envelope and started his engine. It was almost daybreak. He'd drive straight to the office and feed the reports into Cesare to see what it spit out.

4

By the time Sasha pulled into the parking lot at Jordana's campus apartment building, the sun was up. She glanced over at her passenger. The adrenaline had worn off, and Jordana was dozing, curled up with her face partially covered by her jacket hood, the way Java covered his nose with his tail when he slept.

She looked so peaceful that Sasha hated to wake her. Leaving aside the question of how the girl had even managed to fall asleep with several mugs full of caffeine and the sugar bomb of not one, but two, glazed doughnuts coursing through her bloodstream, she had no choice. She needed to get back home, shower, have breakfast with the twins and Connelly and get into the office. No run today. And she'd have to reschedule her Krav Maga workout for lunchtime.

But she was glad Jordana had trusted her enough to call her.

She killed the engine and gave Jordana's shoulder a gentle shake. "Hey, wake up. We're here."

The teenager mumbled and shifted but didn't open her eyes.

She shook her again, less gently this time. "Jordana."

Jordana groaned and turned toward her, bleary-eyed. "Huh?"

"We're at your apartment. I have to get home and get ready for work."

"Oh, yeah. Sorry. Thanks for breakfast," she mumbled as she shoved her feet back into her shoes.

"My pleasure."

She scrubbed her face with her hands. "And thanks for springing me from jail."

She smiled. "Any time."

"Are you sure they're not going to press charges?"

"I'd be surprised. You might get a summary

citation in the mail. If you do, bring it into the office, and we'll take care of it."

Jordana's eyes filled with tears. Sasha blinked. Jordana wasn't a crier, she never had been. She had a tough exterior, much like Sasha's own. But unlike Sasha, the younger woman had never revealed a gooey marshmallow core.

"Hey, you okay?"

Jordana nodded and wiped the tears from her face with an angry motion. "Yeah. I'm just worried about Charlie—Professor Robinson."

"Who's Professor Robinson?" Sasha wrinkled her forehead. Where was *this* coming from?

"He's my Grassroots Organizing prof. He didn't organize the protest or anything, but he knew about it. The leaders invited him to join us, and he did."

"Okay?"

"Professor Robinson and a couple other people got picked up, too, but they weren't on the bus with us, and nobody saw them at the station."

She frowned. "Did you see him get taken into custody?"

Jordana sniffled. "Yeah. They grabbed him first. This black van came careening around the corner, with no lights on. People screamed and dived out of the way. At first, I thought someone was driving into the crowd, you know, like happens sometimes?"

"But that's not what happened?"

"No. The van stopped and all these guys jumped out. All dressed in black, head to toe, with big guns. They were shouting orders, but it was chaos. I don't know what they were saying. I don't think anybody knew. Two of them went straight for Professor Robinson and grabbed him under his arms. They dragged him into the van with a few other people. All guys, nobody I knew well."

Sasha watched her face contort with anguish at the memory. After a moment, she said in a soft voice, "Then what happened?"

"We all kind of stood there in shock. Then Letitia—she's one of the organizers of Justice for Vaughn—ran up to the van and pounded on the window. She was screaming." Jordana's voice shook, and she paused. When she went on her voice was firmer. "They lowered the passenger window and stuck a gun out. Sasha, they put it right into her chest and ordered her to back up. So she did. Then the van sped off. It couldn't have been a minute later when the uniformed police showed up with the school bus."

Sasha chewed on the inside of her lip. It sounded sketchy, no doubt. But Jordana had been through enough for one sleepless night. And it was entirely possible that her professor was home in bed, sound asleep by now.

She reached over and rubbed the younger woman's upper arm. "Do you have class with him today?"

"No. But I know he has office hours from ten until noon."

"Okay. Go get a few hours' sleep. Check his office at ten. If he's not there, text me, and I'll make some calls."

Jordana's tense face crumpled with relief. "Thank you."

"Of course."

"I don't know how I can ever repay you. I have no clue what I would have done if—"

"Hey. We're friends. I would have done the same for Naya, or Will, or Caroline."

Jordana giggled. "Could you imagine Caroline at a protest?"

Sasha smirked. Their office administrator's

polished, high-brow demeanor was genuine. But Sasha knew the woman had another side.

"Adults are more complex than you give us credit for."

Jordana dismissed the notion with an eye roll and a wave of the hand, zipped her jacket up to her chin, and yanked open the car door. Sasha watched her trudge up the wide stone steps to her apartment building and wave her ID in front of the card reader. Once she was inside the glassed-in entryway, Sasha reversed out of the spot and followed the one-way traffic circle through the heart of campus.

It was nearly deserted at this hour. Most of the buildings were still dark and silent. The athletic field was empty. Only the glass library center showed signs of life. Warm lamplight glowed from within, and a row of bicycles stood sentinel in the bike rack in front of the building.

As she passed the entrance at a crawl, too conscious of her sleep deprivation to risk violating the ten-mile-per-hour posted speed, a young guy pushed open the library door and bounded down the stairs toward the bikes.

She slammed on the brakes and stared. Her throat threatened to close, and her brain failed to send the message to her lungs to fill with air. After a breathless moment, she gasped. *Patrick?*

It wasn't Patrick, couldn't be Patrick. Patrick was dead, had been dead for twenty years. She knew—intellectually, of course, she did. But she couldn't pull her eyes away from the young man.

He was Patrick. He didn't *look like* Patrick. He *was* Patrick. He had Patrick's thick, strawberry blond shock of hair. Patrick's smattering of freckles splashed across the bridge of his nose. The squareness of his jaw, the slope over the ears, the broad shoulders and barrel chest—all Patrick's.

Not Patrick as she remembered him when he died, a thirty-year-old man. Adult and serious. This kid was Patrick when he graduated from high school, full of life and possibility and cock-sure swagger.

The teenager skipped the last step and jumped to the ground with a graceful, fluid motion. She stared as he unlocked his bike from the rack and swung one leg over it. He adjusted his backpack and reached for the helmet clipped over his handlebars.

She raised her phone casually as if she were checking directions or a message and snapped a surreptitious picture without looking. She felt vaguely creepy and intrusive, but she needed tangible evidence of this ghost.

He lifted his head and looked directly at her. She froze. *Busted.* Did he know she'd taken his picture? Her brain scrambled, searching for an excuse.

But he gave her a wide, impersonal grin and snapped his helmet strap closed under his chin. As he did so, he lifted his chin and met her gaze, and her breath caught in her throat. Green eyes, her own wide-set green eyes look back at her. The same shape, same emerald hue.

She exhaled and waved him across the crosswalk. He raised a hand in thanks and stood on the bike's pedals, using his momentum to get a good start. The movements were etched in her memory from years of watching Patrick pedal away from the house.

She watched his back grow smaller and smaller and tried to catch her breath, to still her shaking hands, to make sense of what she'd seen.

"You're being ridiculous," she finally said aloud.

Her voice was breathy and trembly in the quiet car. She was seeing ghosts because it was the twentieth anniversary of Patrick's death. Of course, he was on her overtired mind. Twenty years ago today, and she'd been woken by a jarring phone, just as she had been that Saturday in 1999. That's all this was. Any young man with vaguely Irish coloring and the right height and weight would have triggered an emotional response.

Her logical arguments would have swayed a judge, a jury, any reasonable person. But they thudded against her own experience, dull, flat, and unconvincing against what she'd seen with her own eyes: her dead brother was riding a bike around the college campus.

She opened her phone's camera app and studied the picture. It was slightly off center, but in focus. She'd caught him just as he'd raised his head. He stared back at her from under too-long bangs.

"Who are you?" she demanded of the image and half-expected it to answer.

After a long moment, she rolled her eyes and tossed the phone in the center console. *You're exhausted*, she told herself.

She snapped on the radio to drown out her thoughts and headed down the hill.

Patrick is dead. He's dead. Dead.

She repeated the words. They were a mantra, a painful, crushing reminder of reality that weighed on her chest like a stone. But they kept her grounded, tethered to reality. Because the reality was, her brother *wasn't* bicycling around a leafy college campus. He was decomposing in a box deep in the earth in a cemetery across town.

5

Wednesday, November 24, 1999
All Souls Cemetery
Pittsburgh, PA

The cold rain fell harder, and Sasha turned up the collar of her black coat to cover her exposed neck. Next to her, her father gestured for her closest brother to shield her with his umbrella. Sean, staring dead-eyed and unseeing at the sea of the headstones that dotted the hillside, didn't notice.

Dad frowned. She shook her head. It didn't matter. She welcomed the rain—feeling the cold rain that would make her wool coat itch and, later, smell like a wet dog meant that she was alive. Her eyes dropped to the fresh hole in the ground. Unlike Patrick.

Dad shook his head and moved closer to her weeping mother, ensuring that his own black umbrella completely protected his wife.

"There should have been a canopy," Ryan muttered on the other side of Sean. She let his words wash over her, blotting out Father Timothy's intonations.

She noticed that at least the priest was standing under a tarp cover. He wasn't getting wet. And neither was Patrick, snug and dry inside his box. Snug, dry, and soon to be lowered into the gaping hole. Her thoughts came and went as randomly and quickly as the drops falling from the gray sky.

On the other side of her mother, Patrick's wife—er, widow—Karyn wailed.

Poor Karyn. For all the grief she and Ryan and Sean felt, Patrick's wife's searing loss was different. And her parents were feeling something else entirely. Burying their child had hollowed them out, leaving them empty-eyed and pale, stunned.

She turned her neck and craned her head

over her shoulder to catch Allie's eye. She stood between Ryan and Sean's wives, red-eyed and clutching a handkerchief—probably pulled from Riley's bottomless tote bag. Allie nodded at her and flashed a wan smile. She let her gaze drift over Allie's head and fall on Patrick's friends, standing in a clump together. Some of them clung to the hands of girlfriends or wives. Some of them leaned their shoulders against one another in support.

No Cole. Had he wanted to be there, or was he afraid to face her family? Her parents hadn't heard from Cole, at least not as far as she knew, since the night he'd accidentally shot Patrick.

He'd *shot* Patrick. The words punched her in the stomach and took her breath away.

It had been this way all week. She'd sleep-walk through the day in a daze and then—*bam*—something, a song, a phrase, the smell of cinnamon rolls, would hit her and remind her that Patrick was really and truly dead. Shot and killed by his best friend.

Her legs threatened to buckle, and she inhaled deeply.

Keep it together. If you face plant in this mud, Sean'll never let you hear the end of it.

She exhaled—a big whooshing breath—and felt inside her coat collar until her fingers found her necklace. She rubbed her fingers over the spider monkey charm—a gift from Patrick last Christmas.

She and Patrick, the youngest and the oldest. The ten-year age difference only exacerbated their personality differences. They were the yin and yang of the McCandless children. And the only common ground they'd ever found wasn't on the ground at all. It was on the side of a mountain.

She swayed again and gripped the charm. *Just hang on. Don't look down, and don't let go.*

It was advice Patrick had given her once on a sheer rock face. She'd scrabbled ahead of him and gotten herself into a spot where she couldn't reach the next handhold or foothold. She'd dangled there, trapped and on the edge of panic. With over a foot in height on her, Patrick had easily swung to the next hold and then grabbed her, saying, *"Just hang on. Don't look down, and don't let go."*

She made a noise, almost a mewl. It came out soft and small, partially blocked by the boulder of grief lodged in her throat.

Her dad gave her another look, then leaned over and hissed at Sean, "Share your umbrella with your sister. She's gonna catch a cold."

Sean rolled his eyes but inched closer and covered her with his umbrella. She tuned out Father Timothy, the relentless sound of the icy rain, and the image of her brother, still and lifeless, inside a box and let her thoughts drift far away.

Sean brought her back with an elbow to the ribs.

"Hey!"

He cocked his head toward the hole in the ground. Her parents and Ryan looked at her expectantly. Karyn's eyes were pinned on the hole. It was time.

Sasha stepped forward and took the handful of earth the funeral director offered.

As she tossed it on top of the little pile of dirt already on the coffin, Father Timothy intoned, "Ashes to ashes, dust to dust."

She turned away.

As the mourners made their way across the frozen grass, she caught up with Allie and linked her arm through her roommate's.

"Thanks for being here."

Allie turned to face her. She looked awful, almost unrecognizable. Her eyes were swollen and raised red welts stood out on her pale forehead and cheeks.

"Are you okay?"

Allie nodded and turned up the collar of her Burberry trench. "Yeah, I feel silly. Patrick was *your* brother, it's just weird."

"Weird how?"

"I feel ..."

She waited, but Allie didn't go on.

She squeezed Allie's arm. "I get it. My brothers love you. They all think of you as another little sister."

Allie bit down on her lower lip and shook her head. "I don't—"

"I'm sure that does feel weird to you. But you're family."

Of course it would seem strange to Allie. She was an only child, after all.

Allie burst into fresh tears. "I'm sorry."

"It's okay."

It really was. Sasha was trying hard not to shed her own tears, to stay strong for her parents. Allie could cry for both of them.

Allie managed a grateful smile as they reached the row of black limousines.

They slid into the second car and settled in next to Ryan and Riley and across from Sean and Jordan.

"Where's Karyn?" Sasha shook the rain from her hair as she asked the question.

"In the front car with Mom and Dad and Nana," Ryan told her.

Riley and Jordan resumed their conversation across the car.

"I can't believe Cole didn't come."

Sean frowned at his wife. "It's a good thing he didn't. Unless he wants to get his ass kicked."

Jordan twisted her mouth into a frown. "I'm sure he feels awful. It *was* an accident."

"It was stupid is what it was."

Sasha leaned forward. She was itching to know what had happened, but ever since she'd been home, Sean had been close-mouthed and foul-tempered. And her parents clammed up mid-sentence whenever she walked into the room. She was as in the dark now as she'd been on Saturday morning.

"Stupid how? What happened, Sean?"

Jordan flashed her a disapproving look, but

Sean answered in a rapid burst, like he'd been holding the words back through sheer will.

"We were coming out of the Dirty Rocket—it's a nightclub right on the Boardwalk. Pat wanted to get some food. We ran into this group of guys coming the other way, and some tall skinny guy jostled Dale. Words were exchanged."

"Words were exchanged?" Allie echoed in disbelief.

She was obviously not familiar with testosterone-fueled machismo. Sasha's sisters-in-law, on the other hand, were well acquainted with the notion. They rolled their eyes in unison.

Sean went on as if Allie hadn't interrupted. "There was some pushing and shoving. Some swearing. Nothing major. Then one of the guys reached inside his jacket pocket, and Cole yelled 'gun!' Then he whipped out *his* handgun."

It was Sasha's turn to interrupt. "Why'd he have a gun in the first place?"

Sean shook his head. "I don't know. I didn't even know Cole carried. But he aimed across Pat at the kid. Everyone was shouting. Pat grabbed Cole's arm and, I don't know, I guess he jerked Cole's arm up. The gun fired. The bullet hit Pat in the lung."

He fell silent and stared down at his hands.

"The cherry on this crap sundae is that the other guy wasn't even packing," Ryan added in a tight voice.

"What?"

"The other kid, he wasn't going for a gun. He was taking out his mobile phone."

Sasha pressed her hand to her mouth and tried to breathe. Sean was right. Her brother's death *was* stupid. A stupid, avoidable tragedy.

"Pull over, I'm gonna barf," Allie whimpered.

Sean pounded his fist on the divider and called to the driver. The limo came to a stop and Riley flung open the door. While Allie crawled out of the car and hurled, Sasha flopped her head back against the headrest and closed her eyes.

6

Wednesday morning

Charlie rested his forehead against the cold metal bars of the holding cell and tried to work out what time it was. His brain was fuzzy from exhaustion and fear, and he couldn't think.

He turned toward the small square window set high in the concrete block wall and rubbed his temples as he tried to estimate the time of day by the weak sunlight streaming through the dirt-streaked, barred window.

Early morning?

He wished he hadn't dozed off and missed the sunrise, but the long hours of nothingness had pressed in on him and, finally, he'd surrendered to sleep. When he'd closed his eyes the sky had been purple-black, and when he'd opened them, the sun had risen.

In truth, he was grateful for the rest and the reprieve from the unrelenting boredom that had replaced the fear and worry. But now it left him disoriented and wondering. How long until someone reported him missing?

He eyed the other men slumped against the walls, sitting on the floor or curled up on the scattered metal frames that lacked the mattresses they needed to call themselves proper beds.

"Any of you guys know what time it is?" He pitched his voice soft and low so as not to wake anyone who was managing to sleep through part of their captivity.

Were his students lined up outside his office door waiting to pepper him with questions about Howard Zinn and nonviolence and radical honesty? He wondered about them because he didn't dare to let himself think about Raquel. She must be out of her mind with worry. He'd never not come home. In all the years that they'd lived together, he'd never once stayed out all night without calling her. If he was arrested, she was his one call. Always.

But this time, there'd been no call.

He hoped that when he hadn't shown up by morning, she'd had the presence of mind to start calling the local public defenders. Although he was beginning to suspect a PD wasn't going to do him a lot of good, not this time. This was different.

He glanced around the dirty, cold cell. His gaze fell on a rust-colored stain near the drain in the middle of the floor. Had it been made by rusty water, heavy with metals and impurities, or by a past detainee's hot blood pouring out of a wound? After a long moment, he decided he didn't want to know.

Finally, after he'd given up on getting an answer to his question about the time, a long-haired dude in the corner jutted his chin toward Charlie. "I think it's about nine. After eight, for sure."

"Yeah?"

"Yeah. The guards had a shift change while you were sleeping. Figure that was eight o'clock. The sun was up."

It was a reasonable guess. Law enforcement often worked eight to four, four to midnight, and midnight to eight shifts. Sometimes the schedule was six to two, and so on. But if the sun was up, it hadn't been six o'clock when the guards had changed shifts.

"Thanks, man."

"Yeah." The guy jammed his hands in his pocket and glanced away.

Charlie understood. It didn't pay to get too friendly with one's cellmates. Any one of them could decide to cut a deal with the state by providing evidence against you, real or manufactured, to save their own hide. Or, even worse, anyone could be working undercover, planted there specifically to elicit information for the authorities. That was just the way the game was played. And anyone who knew the rules of the game knew not to get suckered.

But hours of boredom and uncertainty won out over Charlie's better judgment, and he found himself edging his way along the cell wall, closer to the guy in the corner.

"Charlie Robinson." He stuck out his hand.

The man stared at it for a long moment

before giving it a quick, reluctant shake. He dropped it like it burned. "Barefoot."

Charlie assumed that was a surname, but Barefoot didn't elaborate.

"Pleased to make your acquaintance, Barefoot."

The guy shook his head. "Nah, man. No offense, but I'm not at all happy to meet you. Not here. Not like this."

Charlie laughed. "Fair point. They pick you up at the protest?"

"Why you want to know? You a reporter or something?"

"No. I'm a professor."

"No crap?"

"True story. I teach a grassroots organizing class, and some of my students put together last night's vigil for Vaughn Tabor. I figured I'd show up in solidarity. I've had lots of time to question the wisdom of that decision."

"You and me both, man." Barefoot nodded.

"Why did you ask if I was a reporter? Did they pick up any journalists last night?"

Not so long ago, Charlie would've been shocked to hear about a reporter getting arrested while covering a peaceful protest. But as the definition of media had expanded to include anybody with a blog or a Twitter account, the First Amendment press protections had dwindled proportionally.

Barefoot didn't respond.

But a skinny kid looked up from examining the dirt under his nails and bobbed his head. "Yeah, they did. I know they grabbed Will Grant from the campus paper and some freelancer for one of the city papers, but they took them to the regular police station. Not ... here."

Charlie recognized the kid from campus. "What's your name?"

"Jackson."

Apparently, first names were taboo in the cellblock.

"Thanks, Jackson. I take it this isn't the Milltown PD, then?"

"Come on, man."

"Yeah."

He'd known from the jump that the Milltown police department had nothing to do with his capture, but he'd been holding out hope that local law enforcement was somehow involved. The alternative was frightening, but not unexpected.

The setup had been wrong from the beginning—from the non-uniformed squad that had scooped them up to the anonymous black van with the rental car company's branded air freshener still hanging from the rearview mirror—the whole thing stank of a covert, off-the-books operation. Federal, if he had to guess. Words like *secret police, unlawful detention, disappeared,* and even *black site* ricocheted around his brain. He suppressed a shudder.

"Cops did show up, though. The regular cops, I mean." Jackson nodded energetically.

"You sure they arrested the press?"

"Yeah. Before they took my phone away, my girl texted me a picture of this school bus that they brought. They were loading people into it. And both the reporters were in line."

"They cuff them?"

"Zip ties. I told Alicia to book it out of there, but I don't know if she got away or not." His eyes fell back to his hands, and he resumed his examination of his nail bed.

Charlie allowed himself to feel a small ripple of relief, despite the weirdness of how it had all gone down. Most likely, most of the protesters had been ordered to disperse. And most of them would scatter. But even the ones who did spend a few hours cooling their heels in a local police department would be okay. Maybe some of them would leave with a fire in the belly and a commitment to the cause. The rest would leave with a story they could tell their old high school buddies when they went home for Thanksgiving break.

Unfortunately, with the immediate pressing worry about his students' well-being lifted, he had nothing to focus on but his own dire circumstances.

"I got a question." Barefoot's voice rang out.

"What's that?"

"Since these guys aren't the cops, and they aren't wearing any federal uniforms, you got any idea who they *are?*"

Suddenly, eight pairs of eyes peered out at Charlie. Looking back at them, he noted with a jolt that the eight faces studying him were all black and brown. There had been plenty of white folks at the protest, but somehow none of them had ended up in the back of the anonymous black van.

Curiouser and curiouser.

"Well? Do you?" Jackson demanded.

Charlie shook his head. He had some suspicions, theories, a couple of guesses. But they were all bad news. Nothing he wanted to give voice to.

"I'm not sure," he finally said.

The uncertainty hung over the room like a heavy cloud, but he was pretty sure knowing would be worse.

7

L eo studied Sasha's face over her bowl of oatmeal. For someone who routinely slept as little as she did, she rarely looked tired. But this morning she seemed ... off. Pale, like a shadow of herself.

For one thing, she'd been unusually quiet. She'd crept back into the house and headed straight for the shower, then spent some time playing with the twins and getting them dressed.

He didn't want to think that she was avoiding him, but he had to wonder. He padded barefoot across the kitchen and filled a fresh travel mug with hot, strong coffee. "I assume you want one for the walk to work?" He asked the question with his back to her.

"Um, yeah, although I'm going to drive today. Do you really need to ask?"

He turned. "No, I guess I don't. Are you sure you can't take a nap before you go into the office?"

She crossed the room to join him at the counter. She dumped her bowl in the sink and filled it with hot water to soak, then gently pried the stainless steel mug from his hand.

"I'm sure. And, really, I'm fine."

"Are you, though? Really?"

She bristled and straightened to her full, meager height. "Of course. How were the kids when they woke up and I wasn't here?"

Changing the subject.

But he answered anyway. "They rolled with it. Easy-peasy."

She arched an eyebrow. "You must have a completely different relationship with our children and pets than I do. Because when I'm playing a zone defense, four on one, I almost never think to describe it as *easy*. Rewarding, even fun, sure. But easy? Not on your life."

He quirked his mouth. The truth was, she held herself to an unrealistically high solo-parenting standard. He, in contrast, had taken the advice of his boss and friend, Hank Richards, single parent to six adopted kids, to heart. The name of the game was survival. Feed 'em, clothe 'em, love 'em. Everything else was gravy. With those goals, it really was easy. Adding elaborate craft projects, foreign language practice, and a sparkling clean house to the mix changed the terrain.

But he wisely shared none of these thoughts with his wife. Instead, he proffered a tray of misshapen balls. "No-bake energy bite?"

"You made these this morning?"

"It was Finn's idea. Fiona supervised. I literally didn't know it was happening until they put me on KP duty."

That admission elicited a genuine laugh from her. She removed the tray from his hands, returned it to the counter next to her to-go coffee, and wrapped her arms around his midsection. She rested her head against his heart.

He pulled her closer. He'd learned that it was sometimes easier to have a conversation with Sasha without making eye contact, especially about difficult topics. So he addressed the crown of her head.

"Today's the twentieth anniversary of your brother's shooting, isn't it?"

She murmured an affirmative answer.

"Are you sure that's not weighing on you?"

She stiffened in his arms for a moment before relaxing back into his chest. "I mean, sure, Patrick's on my mind. And I think Thanksgiving's going to be tough this year. Twenty years. It just feels ... significant. And, I guess, I might've dreamed about it if I was saying Allie's name."

She was telling him the truth. But something in her voice made him think she was holding something back, too.

He lifted her chin with a finger and stared into her bright green eyes. So green that it was startling even after all these years of losing himself in their depths. "You can talk about him, you know."

She blinked and glanced away. "I know." She popped an energy bite into her mouth. "Oh, yeah, I can tell Finn was involved in making these. He has a generous hand with the honey."

"Sasha—"

She forestalled his next line of inquiry by brushing a sweet, sticky kiss against his lips.

He knew what she was doing, of course he

did. But he didn't call her out. He kissed her back, a long, firm kiss.

She took a step back and met his eyes again. "You know who I wonder about?" she asked in a soft voice.

"No. Tell me."

"Karyn—Patrick's wife. They'd been married for eight years when he died. The first couple years she still joined us for the holidays, birthdays. I think she came along for a few Pirates games with the family. But at some point, she started to drift away, and we saw less and less of her. Now I haven't seen her in, oh I don't know, at least a dozen years. I think she still sends my parents a Christmas card, but I don't know where she lives, if she remarried, if she has kids. It's almost like she was never part of the family in the first place. And she *was*—part of the family, I mean. She was a like a big sister. She started dating Pat when I was just a kid."

"You know I don't know a lot about big families."

He suppressed a snort at his own understatement. Raised by a single mom who worked as a traveling nurse, he'd had no siblings and they'd never really put down roots. Hell, it wasn't until after he and Sasha had married and had the twins that he met his father. Family ties were definitely outside his area of expertise.

"Yeah, I know."

He pushed on anyway. "But I could see how, at first, it was probably a comfort to her to be around the McCandless clan, but, as time went on and your other brothers started having babies with their wives, she might have started to feel left behind. It might have been easier for her to fade out of the picture."

She nodded sadly. "You're probably right."

"You could find her if you wanted to. It would probably take Naya three minutes, tops, to track her down, assuming she's not in the Witness Protection Program."

"True. And if she *has* entered witness protection, it might take Naya as long as ten minutes to find her."

She laughed, and the tension around her eyes softened. His heart squeezed.

"You don't always have to be the woman of steel, you know."

For an instant her eyes watered. Then she blinked and, as quickly as they'd filled, they were dry. "I hear you, Connelly, I really do. But I do have too much to do today to have a meltdown. On top of my real work, I promised Jordana that if her professor didn't turn up, I'd I look into it."

He frowned. "Her professor's missing?"

"Maybe. The Milltown police picked up most of the protesters and took them to the station on a school bus. That's where I went to get her. But before the cops arrived, an unmarked black van sped up, and some men dressed in black, no patches or insignias or anything, hopped out and grabbed several men."

"Including the professor?"

"That's what she says. She also says the men in the van were armed to the teeth. I know what you're thinking—that's impossible, right?"

"Seriously? You think *I* would say it's impossible? Me? I'm the guy who works for a shadow agency that doesn't officially exist, remember?"

She furrowed her brow. "You and Hank don't drag civilians off the street at gunpoint." A long pause. "You don't, do you?"

"No, but do I think there's another agency out there that might be? Sure, it's possible. Likely, even."

She blanched. "Fair enough. So, in your

professional opinion, who do you think these men in black are?"

He clicked his tongue against his teeth and thought. "I don't know offhand. But why don't you let me look into this one?"

The last thing he needed was for his wife to start poking around in the dimly lit shadows of federal agencies.

"Okay, but hold off. It may be much ado about nothing. Jordana is supposed to see if her professor shows up for his office hours. She'll text me if he doesn't, and I'll let you know."

"Sounds like a plan." He leaned in for another kiss.

She snagged a handful of the energy bites and was about to dump them in the expensive bag she used as a combination purse/briefcase.

"Stop!" He grabbed a reusable snack pouch from the counter and swept them inside, then pressed the velcro closure shut.

She looked down at the design on the bright yellow fabric. "Um, this is a puppy dog."

"Yes, but our children know better than to throw sticky foods into their backpacks. You need the puppy pouch more than they do."

She stared at him for a few seconds, then

threw back her head and laughed, really laughed. Good grief, but he loved her face when she was unguarded and happy.

"I better run," she said, cutting short the moment. "I love you."

He kissed the top of her head. "I love you more. Take care of yourself today, okay?"

"I always do." She flashed a wide, reassuring grin that did nothing to reassure him. "I mean, I have coffee and energy bites. What more could a girl need?"

He watched as she ruffled Mocha's fur and gave Java a good scratch behind the ears before she headed out to the garage. As she click-clacked away in her high-heeled boots, the answer came to him: sometimes, a girl needed a good long cry. But he didn't know if she'd ever admit as much to herself, let alone admit it to him.

8

L andon pulled into the PPC detention center parking lot, snapped down his sun visor, and stared at himself in the lighted mirror. His eyes were red and blurry, despite the eye drops he'd squeezed into them before leaving the office. And he was exhausted, despite the ice-water bath he'd plunged his face into in the sink of his executive bathroom.

He'd been running on very little sleep for years, for decades, before Josh had died. It was the Silicon Valley way. But after Josh had died, sleep became more than just an interruption and a nuisance. Sleep was the enemy. Sleep kept him from working on Cesare, kept him from creating the program that would stop all the other Joshes from dying.

He knew the consequences. He understood that he was shortening his own lifespan, compromising his health, ruining the quality of his life through chronic sleep deprivation. But none of that was as important as what he did while he was awake. Every hour, every minute, every *second* that he spent perfecting Cesare brought it incrementally closer to achieving its potential. Someday it would be able to predict with great accuracy who would commit a heinous crime before they ever thought of doing it. And it would allow the authorities to stop them, to prevent them. And then, all the exhaustion, the sleepless nights, the misery—it would all be more than worth it.

He snapped the visor closed and took one final look at his revised list. Then he raced from his car to the building with his head bent against the cold wind. He pressed his index finger against the biometric scanner and waited. When the doors opened, he walked inside and relished the blast of hot air that hit him in the face.

He made his way through the labyrinth of

halls on autopilot, following the path that his feet had trod so many times before. When he reached the outer chamber, he squinted at the guard on duty.

"Marshall, right?"

After a moment's pause, the man gave a brisk nod. "Yes, sir."

"I've reviewed the names of the detainees against the files we received from our local law enforcement partners. I've divided the names into two tranches."

He slipped two sheets of paper through the cutout in the bulletproof partition that separated the guard from visitors to the lobby. He waited as Marshall ran his eyes down both short lists.

When he glanced up, Landon continued, "The men on List A are to be blindfolded, driven back to the engagement spot, and dropped off."

"Dropped off?"

"Released."

Marshall tented his brows. "We're just ... letting them go? Sir," he added the honorific quickly to the question in a failed attempt to mask his disapproval.

"Correct. Most of them are students. They

bear watching, and Cesare has flagged their files, but they're not an imminent danger to anyone. The men on List B are the dangerous ones, the ones with established latent criminality."

The guard gave an unconvinced shrug. "You're the expert."

Landon smiled without a hint of warmth. "That I am, Marshall. That I am. Spring List A and then arrange to bring me the men on List B one at a time."

Marshall's eyes widened. "Bring them to you?"

The surprise was warranted; his request was out of the ordinary. Landon did not, as a rule, interact with the latent criminals. But he wanted to probe Cesare's decision-making formula, and the quickest, most effective way to do that was to talk to the men.

"Yes. I'll set up in one of the boxes. Let's say Room B. Bring me the first name on the list once the others have been transferred out of the facility."

He fixed the guard with a steely stare and waited to see how the man would respond. The three boxes in the basement were the only interrogation rooms where every interaction wasn't recorded on both video and audio. Of course, if Marshall were smart, he'd realize that Landon's request itself was being recorded by the overhead camera. And that fact would give him cover if one of the detainees ended up beaten to a pulp, bleeding out in the box.

But Landon saw no reason to make the guard's decision any harder than necessary. It was better, far better, to dispel the worry. He leaned forward, placed his hands face down on his side of the counter, and pitched his voice in a friendly, confidential tone. "I'm just going to talk to them, son. I'll let you hold my weapons while I'm in there."

Marshall nodded, convinced by Landon's reassuring tone and unwavering gaze. "Yes, sir."

Landon removed his Glock from his shoulder holster, and then bent to free his hunting knife from its ankle strap. He pushed both items through the opening. The guard tagged them and dropped them in a metal lockbox.

"There. Now, get started on List A. I'll show myself to Box B."

Without waiting for a response, he strode

toward a heavy metal door to the right of the
reception area and jammed his finger against the
reader. After a short pause, the door beeped and
clicked open. He plunged into the belly of the
building and took the stairs down, down, down
into the dark, dank sub-basement. The bare
overhead lightbulb in the hallway flickered as he
clomped beneath it. He wondered if it was
natural or staged for the horror movie effect.

He reached a door set into the stone wall.
The metal had been coated with flat black paint
and a "B" was scratched into the paint. He
pushed open the door and stepped inside. The
rooms locked from the inside only. The inter-
rogator would throw a heavy, iron sliding bolt
reminiscent of an old-fashioned barn latch
across the door after the suspect was inside the
room. The latch would catch with a deep clang
that echoed off the bare earthen walls. That
detail, he knew, had been chosen for its psycho-
logical effect.

He shrugged out of his suit jacket and
unwound his cashmere scarf, hanging them
carefully over the room's only piece of furniture
—a metal folding chair. Then he rolled his dress

shirt sleeves up to his elbows. Optics mattered in a situation like this. In fact, his five o'clock shadow and his bleary-eyed expression would probably serve him well during his questioning of the men on his list.

He reviewed what he'd learned about the men. Max Barefoot was the most straightforward of the three. An automobile thief for a well-organized black market ring, Barefoot was equally happy to boost parked cars and to take them at gunpoint from their owners. A string of carjackings in the mid-2000s had landed him in the state penitentiary system for a ten-year stint. He'd mostly stayed under the radar since his release, but that didn't mean he was clean. His presence at the protest was puzzling, as he'd not previously shown any signs of activism. Although, Landon allowed, he may have found his calling in the joint. Some men find God behind bars, others reform into social activists. But most of them? They become more hardened versions of the men they were when they entered. Barefoot was a felon. Eventually, he'd commit another felony.

Then there was Sam Blank. His file was

nearly as empty as his surname indicated. Cesare had *not* spit out Samuel Blank's name as a person of interest when the identities of the known protesters were fed into Cesare's facial recognition sequence. But the Milltown police had been adamant that Landon's men pick up Blank as part of the PPC operation.

Why?

The detailed record review shed no light. The man had no real record, save for some vagrancy and loitering charges. The Milltown PD had told Landon there was an outstanding warrant for Blank. It was for public urination, which was a misdemeanor at best. He also had no permanent address. Landon figured the man was either homeless or a gang lookout—the latter of which would explain the hard-on the local police had for him. But he had no known gang affiliations. He was a cipher. A dead end.

Finally, Charles Elijah Robinson, Jr., a professor of grassroots organizing and social justice, of all the ludicrous specializations. He was the wild card of the three. A professional, and yet ... Cesare had flagged him.

Robinson was an adjunct professor, and Landon wondered if his long criminal record played a role in his lack of tenure. He'd been arrested, cited, and given warnings at dozens of protests for innumerable causes. He had no assaults, gun charges, drug charges, or felonies on his record. He did, however, have a decade-old charge for credit card fraud, which he'd pled out, and—not surprisingly—horrendous credit.

Unmarried and childless, the thirty-two-year-old Robinson cohabitated with a woman named Raquel Jones. Robinson and Jones were renters, hopping from apartment to apartment, never laying down roots. Robinson was a registered Independent voter who had dabbled in communism, socialism, and the Green Party. His medical records listed no religious affiliation. He had no known family.

In Landon's experience—and according to Cesare's algorithms—shiftless people like Robinson were volatile. Fiscal irresponsibility was an indicator of a propensity for recklessness. That trait, coupled with a clear disrespect for authority, made Robinson forty-seven percent more likely to commit murder than a financially stable Lutheran who voted but was otherwise not politically active.

Landon intended to use his time with

Robinson to probe for a flash of temper, a hint of violence, something he could use to confirm Cesare's finding. He cracked his neck and rolled his shoulders, then he leaned back against the cold wall, crossed his legs at the ankles, and settled in to wait.

9

A heavy door clanged, rousing Charlie from his catnap. A pair of tall, well-muscled guards prowled down the hallway. They stopped in front of the cell and peered in at the cluster of tired, hungry men through the bars. The guard on the left, who stood maybe a quarter of an inch taller than his partner, looked down at a piece of paper in his hands, cleared his throat, and started reading off names.

"Cover, Adrian; Hernandez, Julio; Jackson, Troy; Marcus, Jayson; Proper, Carter; and Rodriguez, Evan."

The men whose names were read shot one another a series of puzzled, worried looks. Then, one by one, they stepped forward, inching toward the bars. Jackson, whose first name was evidently Troy, licked his lips, a quick, nervous movement, and craned his neck toward Charlie.

Jackson didn't speak, but his eyes pleaded with Charlie to find out what was going to happen to him. He eyed the six men queuing up at the front of the cramped cell. They were all young. In their late teens or early twenties. Students, probably. First-time protesters, maybe. Scared witless and afraid of making a mistake.

He nodded to the second guard, a light-skinned guy with a shaved head and the shoulders of a linebacker. "Hey, my brother, what's going on?"

The guard narrowed his eyes, an almost imperceptible expression of disdain. He answered Charlie's question with one of his own. "Did Officer Fox read off your name?"

"No."

"Then it's not your concern, *my brother.*"

Fox laughed. Charlie felt the quick surge of anger in his chest and flexed his hands. Once, twice. *Release it. Let it go.*

He tried for a placating tone. "I'm a professor

at the college. Some of these young men are students. It's my duty to look out for—"

"It's a little late to act *in loco parentis*, don't you think, Teach?" Fox smiled at him, baring his teeth.

In loco parentis was a term of art in higher education ... and the law. Who *were* these guys?

"Officer, I'm just seeking some assurance that their rights are not going to be violated."

He left unsaid the fact that the constitutional rights of every man in the cell had been trampled a dozen different ways from the moment the black van careened into the vigil.

Fox's partner spoke up. "You don't need to worry about your students' rights. *They're* being cut loose." He jammed an oversized iron key into the lock and the metal bars swung open with a groan.

"Let's go," Fox barked.

Troy darted out of the slow-moving line and grabbed Charlie's wrist. "What should I do? Tell a dean or something?"

"No. Go to my department and find my teaching assistant, Rush Winters. Explain what happened. He'll know what to do. And Troy, ask him to call Raquel for me."

"Got it."

He released Charlie's wrist. Charlie grabbed his hand and shook it. Troy nodded and slipped back into the line.

When the last man in line was clear of the cell's entrance, Fox withdrew the key, and the door slammed shut with a click that echoed. Charlie watched as the group shuffled down the hall and passed out of sight. He turned back to the two other men who remained in the cell: Barefoot and a slight, watchful man who—as far as Charlie knew—hadn't spoken a word since they'd been picked up.

Barefoot's mouth twitched. "Well, this is bad."

"Yep."

The third man's eyes darted between Charlie's face and Barefoot's.

"Do you know him?" Charlie cocked his head toward the guy.

"Nah. He doesn't talk."

"I noticed."

"So it's probably safe to talk in front of him, you know what I mean?"

Charlie studied the man's face. He stared back at Charlie.

"You okay, man?"

The guy shifted his gaze to Charlie's mouth as he asked the question. Lip reading. He nodded.

Charlie signed, *"My name is Charlie. This is Barefoot."* His fingers were thick and clumsy, but the language came back to him as soon as he started moving them.

The man signed back his name, finger-spelling it so quickly that Charlie almost missed it. *Sam.*

"What's that you're doing? Flashing gang signs?"

Charlie bit back his sarcastic response. "No, we're using sign language. His name is Sam."

"Tell him I'm Barefoot."

"I did. But I think Sam can also read lips, so if you face him when you talk, you can tell him yourself."

"Cool." He turned to face Sam. "What'd they pick you up for?"

Sam started to answer, then paused, his hands hovering while he thought. After a moment, he went on.

Charlie interpreted for Barefoot, hoping his rusty skills were enough to allow him to recount

Sam's story faithfully. "He went to the vigil. He knew the dead boy and wanted to pay his respects. He says he has an outstanding warrant."

Barefoot's eyes flashed.

"Do you, too?"

"Do I what?"

"Is there a warrant out for you?" Charlie asked in a mild voice.

"No."

"Huh. Me neither. I'm trying to figure out why the three of us are still here, what we have in common."

Barefoot flared his nostrils. "Well, I'm not a college professor. And I'm not a deaf guy with a warrant, so I don't know what to tell you."

Charlie thought back to their first exchange. Barefoot had kept track of time by noticing the shift change.

"Have you done time?"

Barefoot shot back instantly, aggression masking defensiveness. "Yeah, I did a stint. You?"

Sam followed the exchange, judging by the surprise that sparked in his eyes.

"No." He figured radical honesty was his best chance of creating an alliance. He signed for

Sam as he explained to Barefoot, "But I do have an old charge for credit card fraud. I pled out, but it's there. And I've been arrested plenty—at demonstrations, protests, sit-ins, that sort of thing."

His first arrest had come when he was just in middle school, at a protest against the World Bank and the International Monetary Fund, and the arrests had continued apace. The arrests had not—until now, at least—involved being abducted off the street by armed men with no obvious law enforcement affiliation and being held in an undisclosed location.

Sam hesitated. He positioned himself so his back was to the ceiling-mounted camera. His chest heaved and he signed, "I saw it."

"You saw it? You saw what?"

His fingers trembled. "The boy. Vaughn. I was there when they killed him. I ran. But they know I saw."

Holy sh—

"What's he saying?" Barefoot demanded.

"He was there when the police killed Vaughn Tabor. He took off, but the cops know he saw it."

"Aw, man, we're fu—"

The metal door at the end of the hallway

banged open, and Barefoot trailed off mid-profanity. Fox and his partner were back. Barefoot dropped his eyes to his dirty fingernails, and Sam jammed his hands into his pockets.

"Come on, professor. You're up first." Fox's grin prickled the back of Charlie's neck.

"Up first for what?"

Fox laughed. "You wanna tell him, Scott?"

"With pleasure. You're going into the box. Now step up to the bars and turn around."

For an immeasurable moment, he considered refusing. Reckless though the idea was, it felt safer than obeying. But Raquel's face flashed in his mind. Her big, sorrowful eyes, the worry lines in her forehead, the tremor of her lower lip. And he trudged to the front of the cell on lead-encased feet and turned his back.

Charlie stood rigidly still while Scott wrapped the belly chain around his waist and padlocked it behind his back. Scott moved around to Charlie's front and pulled his right wrist across his stomach to the handcuff on his left and secured it, then cuffed his left wrist to his right side. Finally, Fox shackled Charlie's ankles into the leg irons that connected to the belly chain via another length of chain.

"Aw, c'mon, man. This is some Hannibal Lecter-type mess right here," Barefoot protested.

His outburst caught Charlie off guard. Then Charlie caught a glimpse of Sam's stricken face and understood. Barefoot and Sam knew they could be next. They were scared. Barefoot might hide it under bluster, but they were both scared.

Unable to move his hands to sign that he was okay, Charlie locked eyes with Sam and spoke slowly, enunciating each syllable. "Nah, man. No muzzle."

Barefoot barked out a laugh. Sam managed a thin smile.

Fox and Scott were less amused. Scott pushed him forward, and he stumbled into the cell bars.

As he shuffled along the hallway, his facade crumbled. He was scared, too.

10

S asha scrolled through the screens of electronic discovery, searching for the keywords that would establish that her client had not deliberately engaged in price-fixing behavior with a cabal of competitors. Her focus was split between the sales team's emails and the ghost she'd seen earlier.

Stop thinking about Patrick.

She rolled her neck and took a sip of not-quite warm enough coffee then dove back into the communications.

Concentrate on the task at hand. Distraction is your enemy. Her Krav Maga instructor's voice echoed in her mind.

Funny how she seemed to apply Daniel's self-defense strictures to her legal work and legal reasoning to her hand-to-hand combat drills. But it worked. For her, at least. Just last week, she'd used her trial attorney's ability to read people to predict that Daniel's elbow strike was a feint and dodged the real blow neatly. *A witness's body always tells the truth, especially when his mouth is telling lies.*

"Seriously, pay attention," she muttered aloud to herself.

A soft rap on her door rescued her from the task at hand. She raised her head to see her partner and best friend, Naya Andrews, standing in the doorway with two oversized ceramic mugs.

"My savior!"

Naya beamed and stepped inside. "I ran down to Jake's for a mocha-pumpkin-cider-something and figured you could use a fresh coffee."

"Always. You're a goddess." She took the warm mug and flashed Naya's mug a skeptical look. "Is that whipped cream?"

"With caramel drizzle." Naya licked the topping and eyed Sasha defiantly. "Say something. I dare you."

"Carl's still on his sugar-free kick, huh?"

Naya grumbled. "That man. It's gearing up to the holidays, as anyone who's been subjected to your incessant Christmas song playlists for the past month can attest. Who on earth cleans up their diet in November? Save that stuff for the new year."

Sasha made a noncommittal *hmm* sound.

That first week of Carl's clean-eating kick, the sugar-free Naya had been scary. At times, terrifying. Then she'd discovered that Jake's specialty drinks were basically desserts in a mug. So, she drank her sucrose and made a big show of telling Carl that she'd sworn off Jake's brownies and cookies. On balance, the subterfuge seemed worth it. Will no longer dove under his desk when he saw Naya coming.

She turned down her music and sipped the hot coffee. "Ah, I needed this. Thanks."

Naya perched on the edge of Sasha's desk with her confection. She peered at the screen. "Car-o-Tech discovery?"

"Yeah."

"Please tell me they didn't memorialize any price-fixing plans via email?"

Sasha pulled a face. "If they did, I haven't found it ... yet. But, you know if they did it, someone was reckless enough to put it in writing."

"Mmm-hmm."

"So far, a pair of the Northeastern Region sales reps *have* committed the details of their extramarital affair to email."

Naya grimaced. "Yuck. Any porn yet?"

"What do you think?"

"There's always porn," Naya marveled, shaking her head. "At work. What are people thinking? I can't say I miss document review."

"Different strokes, I guess. I'd rather wade through grimy details of affairs and wish for mind bleach than stare cross-eyed at due diligence documents for some private offering or whatever it is you're doing in there while you listen to musical soundtracks on a loop."

"*Hamilton* will see a girl through a lot—including a round of angel investing. But I won't lie, I was falling asleep. We need some more junior associates to do this grunt work."

Sasha shrugged. She wasn't wrong. "Talk to Will. That's his job. I do have something more exciting for you, if you want to liven things up a bit."

Her face brightened. "Yeah?"

"Yeah. Wanna play internet detective?"

"You know it." She abandoned the drink and rubbed her hands in anticipation. "Hit me."

Sasha scrawled Karyn's full name and last known address on a bright purple sticky note, pulled it off the pad with a flourish, and passed it to Naya. "Can you find this woman?"

"Karyn Bishop. Any aliases?"

"Karyn McCandless."

Naya's eyes snapped up from the note. "Any relation?"

Sasha cleared her throat. "She was married to Patrick."

Naya's expression didn't change, but one perfectly shaped eyebrow shot up her forehead. "They were together when he ... it happened?"

A quick nod. "Yeah. Bishop was her maiden name. I don't know whether she's still using McCandless or if she remarried or what. But I figured her maiden name would be a solid way to track her down."

"It should. She still live at this address?"

"Honestly? I doubt it. It was a fixer-upper in Dormont. And Patrick did almost all the fixing-up himself, with his buddies. If I were Karyn, I would have made it livable and sold it ages ago."

Naya eyed her sidelong. Her eyes flickered under her long, thick, enviable eyelashes. She said nothing.

"What?" Sasha demanded.

Naya stared down into her drink. "Nothing."

"Clearly it's something."

"It's none of my business. But ... why are you looking for this woman *now*? Isn't it the ..."

"Twentieth anniversary of Patrick's death?"

"Yeah."

Sasha leaned forward, itching to spill the burden of what she'd seen, to tell someone what she'd seen. *Who* she'd seen.

Before she could unburden herself, Jordana burst into the room, pale and shaky.

"Sasha! I need you to come to campus with me. Now." She was trembling with urgency.

Naya cocked her head. "What the ...? You know what? I don't want to know. I got this." She slipped the note into the pocket of her dress and gave it a pat. As she picked up her coffee and hurried out of the office, Sasha made a mental note to ask Naya where she found all those pocketed dresses.

Naya stopped and grasped Jordana by the shoulders. "You okay, Jay?"

Jordana shook her head no while she said, "Yes."

The lack of synchrony was a classic tell that she was lying. Naya caught it, too. She turned and gave Sasha a *look* before heading out and closing the door behind her.

"What's the matter? You look awful."

"I went to Professor Robinson's office like you said."

"He's not there?"

"No. And when I got there, this kid from my French class was talking to the teaching assistant and, well, I think you should talk to Troy yourself. I tried to get him to come here with me. But he's too freaked out."

Sasha frowned and started packing up her bag. She wanted to ask why Jordana hadn't just called her, but experience had taught her that sometimes people didn't act rationally when they were under stress. Especially when those people were teenagers or young adults whose brains were still developing.

Besides, going to the campus would give her a chance to look for Patrick's doppelgänger again. She wished that hadn't been her first thought, but it had. She drained her coffee and snapped off her office light.

"Okay, let's go."

TROY JACKSON PERCHED on the corner of the sofa in Charlie Robinson's cramped office. His right knee bounced up and down as he jiggled his leg. Rush Winters, the professor's TA, a bird-like, wiry man with a mop of unruly hair and square hipster eyeglasses, stood behind the professor's desk, wringing his hands.

Jordana made the introductions and collapsed onto the sofa next to Troy. If Sasha had to guess, the only sleep the girl had gotten had been her catnap in the car on the way home from the police station.

She dragged a guest chair from in front of the desk across the room, positioning it directly in front of Troy. She seated herself, dug a legal pad and pen out from her bag, balanced the pad on her thigh, uncapped the pen and wrote the date on the top sheet, then locked eyes with Troy.

"Troy, tell me exactly what happened. I'm

going to ask you to go through it once without interruption. Then I'll ask questions, okay?"

He nodded his understanding. Before he could start, Jordana interjected with a question. "Do Rush and I need to leave? If this is privileged?"

It was a smart question, and Sasha didn't hide her proud smile.

"At this point, there's no attorney-client relationship between Mr. Jackson and me, so this conversation wouldn't be confidential whether you were here or not. Do you think you need an attorney, Troy?"

He took his time answering. But after a moment, he gave a slow shake of his head. "Nah, I don't think so. They didn't charge me with anything."

"Great. So for now, Jordana and Rush can stay in the room, unless you'd rather speak in private?"

Troy glanced sidelong at Jordana, and his leg stilled as if her being there calmed him. "I'd like them to stay."

"All right. Then let's get started. You were at the protest last night?"

"Yeah. Um, yes, ma'am."

"You don't need to be formal with me. So, I guess start from the point when the black van arrived on the scene." She smiled to encourage him to relax.

He swallowed hard, his Adam's apple bobbing, and took a long drink of water. "Okay. I was there with my, uh, girlfriend. We were standing next to each other when this van sped around the corner and screeched to a stop. At first, I thought they were planning to plow into the crowd, you know? I pushed Alicia behind me. People scrambled in every direction. Then the doors fly open and a bunch of big guys jump out. There must've been six of them, maybe more. All dressed in black. Black boots, black pants, long-sleeve shirts under vests. Three of them had guns. Uh, assault rifles, I guess. They dragged me into the van, zip-tied my hands together in front of me. It happened fast."

He paused and sipped some more water. Jordana gave his shoulder a sympathetic squeeze. The TA peeked at his cell phone and made a small noise.

"Sorry to interrupt, but the professor's partner just texted me. I left her a message this morning to let her know what's going on. She wants me to call her. What should I tell her?"

Sasha's priority was getting the whole story out of Troy while it was still fresh in his memory. "Text her back and tell her you'll call her in twenty minutes, maybe less." She returned her attention to Troy while Rush thumbed out the message. "So they put you in the van."

He passed his hand over his eyes before answering. "Right. I was the second one in. There were nine of us all together. Just kind of thrown in the cargo hold, bouncing around. I still had my phone in my hands, so I texted Alicia before they took it. It was dark in there, so I couldn't really recognize anybody. We drove for a while, I don't know how long. I think we were on the highway for a while because we were going pretty fast. Then we slowed down and the road got real bumpy."

She broke her own rule to ask for clarification. "Bumpy like it wasn't paved?"

He scraped his teeth over his upper lip and considered the question. "No, not like that. It wasn't like going over loose gravel or packed dirt that had ruts. More like ... cracked and broken road. A lot of potholes."

Great. Poorly maintained with potholes. That ought to narrow it down to ... almost every secondary road in Western Pennsylvania.

She looked down at her scribbled notes. She had so many follow-up questions already, but she really did want to hear him tell it through once unprompted. She worried that her questions would shape the narrative. She'd just have to limit her questions as best she could.

"Go on, Troy. You're doing great."

"The van stopped. They blindfolded us and marched us into some building. We were stumbling and tripping. They put us in a cell and removed the blindfolds. That was the first time I got a good look at the other guys. And that's when I recognized the professor."

"Did you recognize anyone else?"

"Yeah, a couple, just from seeing them around campus."

"Were they all students?"

He shook his head. "Most of us, yeah. Two dudes were older—besides Professor Robinson, I mean. One of the guys said his name was Barefoot. The other guy didn't say a word all night."

"Okay. What happened next?"

Troy raised both shoulders to his ears.

"Nothing. Not for a long time. Nobody questioned us or anything. We didn't get a phone call or any food or water. We just kinda ... sat there for hours. In the morning, two guards came and read off everyone's names except the professor's, that Barefoot guy, and the quiet one. They blindfolded us again and led us out to a vehicle. I think it was the same van, but I'm not sure about that. They drove us back to the protest site and gave us back our phones and stuff, then took off the blindfolds and rolled out."

"Did you catch a license plate ... even partial?"

"It was covered with mud. I mean covered—like somebody painted it on."

Intentional. Organized. Cruelly efficient.

"And these men never identified themselves as members of a law enforcement agency?"

"Nope."

"Your professor, Mr. Barefoot, and the silent man are still being held?"

He blinked rapidly. "Far as I know."

"Did you catch any of the other students' names?"

"Yeah. But ... nobody else wanted to get

involved. Everyone kind of wants to pretend it never happened."

An understandable, if regrettable, impulse. She'd leave it alone. For now.

She reached into her bag and withdrew a business card. "Thanks a lot for talking to me, Troy. If you think of anything else, call me."

He palmed the card and hurried to his feet, eager to get out of there. "Yeah, okay. Are you gonna help him?"

"I'm going to try." She turned to the teaching assistant. "We'll call his partner together. I'm going to offer to represent her to figure out where he is and who's holding him and then get him released."

Troy was heading for the door.

"Troy, wait a minute."

He turned back, his eyes wary. "Yeah?"

She took out her phone and pulled up the picture she'd snapped earlier. "Do you know this guy?"

He leaned toward the display and studied the face that had stopped her heart. After a long moment, he shook his head. "Sorry, no."

She'd known it was a long shot that he would, but still, her chest grew heavier. "Thanks anyway. And thanks again for coming forward to help Professor Robinson."

"Sure thing. Bye, Jordana."

"See you later." Jordana stretched her neck to peer at the phone in Sasha's hand as Troy left the room.

Sasha handed her the phone. "Do you recognize him?"

"No. I mean, he looks familiar ... but ... no. Is he involved?"

"No. I just saw him on campus this morning and need to track him down. It's for an unrelated matter."

Jordana wrinkled her brow and passed the phone to Rush. "Do you know him?"

He studied the image and returned the phone to Jordana. "Sorry. I can't say that I do."

Jordana glanced down at it again before handing it back to Sasha. "You know what's funny?"

"No, what?"

"For some reason, he reminds me of Finn."

Sasha's heart crashed into her stomach and a wave of grief rolled over her. She took a deep breath and managed a weak smile. "That's strange."

Jordana bounced on her toes. "So now what?"

"Now, Rush and I will talk to the professor's significant other. Then I'll get to work. I promise you the firm will do everything we can to help Professor Robinson. What *you* need to do now is go back to your apartment and get some sleep."

"But—"

"No buts about it. You've had a grueling eighteen hours. Rest. Hydrate. Eat. That's your job."

Defiance flashed in Jordana's eyes, but, after a moment, she acquiesced. "I am pretty beat."

"Go on. Take care of yourself."

Jordana shuffled out of the office.

Sasha turned to the teaching assistant. "Okay, let's make that call."

Before Rush could pull out his phone, someone pounded hard on the office door. He raised his eyebrows as he went to open it. He wasn't more than halfway across the room when the door flew open.

"What the—?"

Three uniformed police officers rushed into the office. Sasha leapt to her feet.

"Out," the lead officer ordered. She had short silver hair and a tired expression.

Sasha narrowed her eyes. "I know you. Officer Diamond, right?"

The woman must've just passed Jordana in the hallway, but she gave no sign of recognition that Sasha had picked the girl up from the police station just hours ago.

"Out," she repeated.

"I beg your pardon?"

The other two officers had begun to prowl around the office, pawing through the professor's papers and books, opening drawers, and sweeping files onto the floor. Rush threw Sasha a panicked look.

"I said out. O-u-t. We're conducting a search of these premises, and you need to leave," Officer Diamond informed her.

Sasha drew herself up to her full (almost) five feet. "Wait just a minute. This isn't how you execute a lawful search. One, you're outside your jurisdiction. Two, where's the warrant?"

"This isn't your office, is it?" Diamond asked in a tone that made clear she knew the answer.

"No, but—"

"And I know it's not *his*," the officer hissed, pointing at Rush, who visibly withered under her attention.

"I'm an attorney," Sasha shot back. "I represent Professor Robinson."

"Is that so?"

"Yes." *Sort of.*

"I don't suppose you have a copy of a signed representation agreement on you?" She waited a beat. "Didn't think so."

"Call his partner. She'll tell you."

Officer Diamond lost what little patience she'd exhibited. "I'm not calling his partner or his mommy or his daddy. Unless you can produce evidence that you represent the man himself *or* Professor Robinson shows up and says you're his lawyer, you have no business here, and you need to leave."

Rush was already scurrying out the door. Sasha glared at his back, then said, "This is an illegal search. It's pointless. Anything you find here will be excluded from evidence, you know that, right?"

The officer leafing through the books on Charlie's bookshelf turned and laughed. "That's a good one, eh, Diamond? The exclusionary rule, right."

"I *am* right. Evidence obtained in violation of the Fourth Amendment protections against unreasonable search and seizure isn't admissible," Sasha insisted.

"Thanks for the free legal advice, counselor. Ever hear of the inevitable discovery exception? Now, for the last time, I'm asking you to leave. If you don't, these gentlemen will escort you out."

Sasha gritted her teeth and stormed out of the office to find Rush.

11

Landon straightened up at the knock on the door.

"Bring him in," he called.

Fox and Scott pushed Charlie Robinson inside. He stumbled and tripped, landing hard, his knees smashing down into the cement floor. The door clanged shut, and the guards departed, their laughter echoing off the earthen walls as they clomped down the hallway.

Landon watched impassively as Robinson struggled to his feet. It was a laborious process, given that he was essentially strait-jacketed. He ended up walking on his knees to the corner and sliding his back up the wall, panting. When he was finally standing and relatively steady, he glared at Landon.

"I'd offer you a seat, Mr. Robinson. But, as you can see, there's only the one." He waved an airy hand around the bare room.

"Who are you?" Robinson demanded when he'd caught his breath.

"That's not important."

"What is this place—a black site?"

Landon rolled his eyes. "You leftists can be so dramatic with your language. I assume your question is whether this is an official federal facility? And the answer is no, it is not."

"What is it then?"

He deliberated over his response. "For your purposes, it's enough to know that I oversee a beta program that interfaces with federal and local law enforcement across the nation. This is one of our facilities."

The professor narrowed his eyes. "A beta program, huh? Are you perfecting how best to deny people their constitutional rights or what?"

"Now, now. Surely you're not suggesting that you been tortured or beaten?"

"Uh, no. At least not yet."

"Deprived of sleep, then?"

He huffed. "Not actively. Your thugs didn't blare music or flash the lights. But, as I'm sure you know, there aren't any cots or pillows or anything in that cage."

"Ah, so our accommodations aren't up to your standards. How unfortunate." Landon was surprised at how much he enjoyed toying with this man.

"I *have* been denied food, water, and the opportunity to call counsel."

"Counsel? You haven't been arrested. As I'm sure *you* know, you're not entitled to an attorney absent an arrest."

Robinson flared his nostrils. "What do you want, man? Why am I here?"

"Now, there's a question I'm happy to answer. You're here because we've determined you have a propensity toward violent crime."

The man's mouth popped open to form a small 'o' of surprise. A moment later, he clamped his mouth shut and jutted his chin forward. He stared hard at Landon. "Nuh-uh, no way. I've never been charged with a violent crime."

"Ah, that's true. I didn't say you had. I said that we've determined you have a propensity for violent crime."

MELISSA F. MILLER

"Determined on what basis?"

"That's proprietary."

"This is ridiculous. I'm a college professor."

"I know. I know quite a bit about you. You're a professor of social justice—a radical. You are unmarried, but you live with a woman named Raquel Jones. Tell me, is she a girlfriend or just a roommate?"

"She's my partner. Not everyone needs a piece of paper from the state to make it official."

"How predictable."

Anger flashed in his eyes. "Keep her name out of your mouth."

Landon noted the reaction. Robinson's woman was a delicate topic; this was useful information. He moved on. "Let's talk about your credit card fraud."

A snort of disbelief. "Are you serious? That was a decade ago. I was broke, and a housemate used my card without permission, ran it up over the limit. I couldn't pay the bill, so I told the bank the charges weren't authorized. Because they *weren't*. But when they investigated and found out that the charges were made by a friend, they told me I had to file a criminal complaint against him or they would file one against me."

Landon telegraphed his disbelief with a sneer. "And I'm to believe you're such a man of honor that you took the fall rather than implicate a friend who was clearly willing to screw you over?"

"I'm telling you, it was an unauthorized use of my card. But, yeah, I wasn't going to sell him out to save myself. So, they filed, and the district attorney offered me a plea deal. And I didn't have the resources to fight the charges, so yeah, I pled out. *That's* why you're holding me in this dungeon? Over an eight-thousand-dollar credit card bill?"

"In a nutshell, yes. A very sophisticated program identified you as a person with latent violent criminality. I take that seriously."

"Well, your program's flawed. It's crap."

"Cesare is not crap." Landon fisted his hands. As soon as he realized what he'd done, he relaxed his fists and shook out his hands.

"Cesare? Who's Cesare?"

Pull yourself together, Landon. Do not allow yourself to be baited.

He ignored the question. "The nine of you whom the agents removed from the protest were the most dangerous based on our preliminary data. But additional information and finer determinations resulted in the release of the six students. Would you care to know why?"

"You're going to tell me whether I want to know or not. You obviously love the sound of your own voice."

"I believe part of the distinction is that the six men deemed a lesser threat are all younger and enrolled in college. That opens up more opportunity for them. The fact that the program didn't seem to adjust for your status as a college educator surprised me at first. But I believe your radical political views likely counteract any 'sweetener' that would be applied for a white-collar job in higher education."

Robinson smirked. "My political views, huh? You sure that's what your fancy program bases its determination on?"

"What's that supposed to mean?"

"I couldn't help noticing that there weren't any white people thrown into that van by your jackbooted thugs. And no women either. The scary Black and brown man stereotype isn't exactly cutting edge. It's pretty worn out at this point, don't you think?"

Landon gritted his teeth. He'd also noted the

skewed demographics, but he'd calibrated the scoring criteria himself and was quite sure there was no bias.

He opened his mouth to argue with Robinson, but caught himself in time. "I don't need to explain my methods to you."

"Your big top-secret program's racist. That's cool."

"Ces—the program can't be racist, professor. It's a series of ones and zeros."

"Sure, whatever you say."

Landon's pulse shot up. He could feel it throbbing in his neck. He shot out of the chair and advanced on the shackled man. "You might want to rein in your derision, Professor Robinson. You are, after all, in a vulnerable position." He grabbed Robinson's collar and shook him.

Robinson's smirk vanished. "And you say *I'm* the one with latent violent tendencies?"

Landon exhaled and dropped his hands to his side. "So, your cellmates, Mr. Barefoot and Mr. Blank—what do you think of them?"

"Oh, I get it. You think I'm the most likely to snitch because I've got a professional job. Sorry, man. I'm not your weak link."

"Really?"

"Yeah, really. Weren't you listening? I told the credit card company to get stuffed rather than turn on my roommate."

"Your loyalty to two total strangers is touching. I wonder, then, who might be interested in talking to me. Mr. Barefoot is an ex-con, so he, presumably, knows firsthand how valuable information can be to law enforcement. I could see him being amenable to snitching, as you say."

Landon caught the shadow of uncertainty that passed over Charlie Robinson's face. Robinson thought Barefoot might be capable of it. He probed further.

"But I'm more intrigued by Samuel Blank. What do you think he might have to say?"

He searched Robinson's face. It was expressionless. Too expressionless.

Robinson dropped his gaze and shrugged awkwardly, his wrists still bound to his hips and his chains jangling. "No idea."

"I think he's my weak link," he bluffed. "I predict Mr. Blank's going to sing like the proverbial canary."

Robinson snorted. "Doubt it." After a beat, he went on, "You know he's deaf, right?"

"I beg your pardon?"

"Sam. He's deaf, and he doesn't speak. So unless you have someone in this squalid pit who knows sign language, you're not going to be able to question him about anything, let alone get him to squeal." Amusement danced in Robinson's eyes.

Rage bubbled up; Landon felt his blood coursing through his veins, hot and fast. His face heated. The Milltown PD should have told him. He couldn't possibly locate a qualified ASL interpreter on no notice. Any third-party contractor would have to be thoroughly vetted, pass a security clearance, and sign a nondisclosure agreement. He needed lead time.

He growled. "And you know this how?"

Robinson hesitated. "I can sign a little. My auntie lost her hearing as a kid. Scarlet fever. My mom taught me so I could talk to her."

The knot of anger in Landon's chest loosened. He bared his teeth. "Your aunt's loss is my gain. You'll interpret."

He expected instant capitulation, but his prisoner surprised him. Charlie Robinson raised his head and stared at him, eyes ablaze.

"I'll do it. On one condition. I get a phone call first. I want to speak to Raquel. Otherwise, you can do what you have to, but I won't help you."

Landon didn't like it, but that's what compromise felt like: everyone was equally unhappy. Robinson had leverage, and he knew it.

He sighed. "Five minutes. No more."

12

Sasha was backing her station wagon into a spot in the lot behind the offices when her cell phone rang. She glanced at the display and accepted the call.

"Hi, Naya."

"Hey, Mac, I found your brother's widow."

Sasha was adept at electronic research, quite adept. But Naya was better.

"That was fast."

"She wasn't hiding. That makes it easy."

Sasha killed the engine, slung her bag over her shoulder, and got out of the car. She hit the remote lock and headed toward the building. "Still, I owe you one. I just pulled in. I'm on my way up to the office. Want me to stop at Jake's

and get you another one of those frothy abomi-
nations? My treat."

Naya groaned. "Pass. I think I'm getting a
cavity from all the ..."

"Sugar?"

"Bite your tongue. Stop by my office when
you get up here. I'll give you what I have on
Karyn Fletcher."

"Fletcher? She remarried?"

"Yeah."

"Okay. See you in two."

She slipped into the building through the
employee entrance and took the back stairs two
at a time. Her heels clattered against the wood
steps and her heart clattered against her rib cage.
Karyn had remarried?

She reminded herself that it had been two
decades since Patrick's death. But still ... the
news made her pulse flutter and her palms go
clammy.

She tried to imagine starting a new life if,
Heaven forbid, Connelly were to die, and her
ordinarily overactive imagination failed her.

She waved a greeting to Caroline, who was
leaving Will's office, and ducked into Naya's. The
windows were cracked, letting in a rush of late

autumn air. The room had to be sixty degrees, at most. She eyed Naya's flushed face and decided not to comment on the temperature. Carl had confided that one of the reasons he'd declared the month a sugar- and alcohol-free one was that Naya was going through "The Change," and he'd read that avoiding sugar and booze might help her symptoms.

Sasha thought it was achingly adorable that he'd done the research and launched a mission, but they both knew Naya would murder them in cold blood if she found out that they'd discussed her menopausal state behind her back, so Carl had sworn her to secrecy and she readily agreed.

"Thanks again for doing this for me," she chirped as Naya fanned herself with a legal journal.

"No problem. Here's what I found." Naya swiveled her chair around to pluck a thick printout from the printer. She clamped a binder clip around the stack of papers and handed the bundle to Sasha.

Sasha flipped through the information, scanning more than reading. Karyn Fletcher, formerly Karyn McCandless, nee Karyn Bishop, resided in the northern suburb of Franklin Park with her husband Brinkley Fletcher and their three children, Britt, Brad, and Brianna, ages ten, seven, and five. Karyn was a stay-at-home mom. Brinkley worked as a pharmacist.

"These kids are all too young," Sasha mused.

"Too young for what?"

She blinked. She hadn't meant to say that aloud. She hesitated, searching for a plausible lie, but Naya was giving her the stink eye.

"To be Patrick's."

"Well, yeah. Karyn didn't marry her second husband until 2007. The oldest was born two years later."

Sasha nodded.

Naya crossed her arms over her chest, pinned Sasha with a look, and waited.

Sasha looked back at her blankly for nearly half a minute, then sighed and dropped the printout into her bag. She took out her phone and pulled up the picture of the kid she'd seen in front of the library. She handed it to Naya, who studied it for a moment.

"So? He kind of puts me in the mind of Fiona. Who is he?"

Sasha nodded toward Naya's computer.

"Search for the 1987 District All-Star Baseball Team. There should be a Post-Gazette article."

Naya's fingers flew over the keyboard. "Got it."

"Enlarge the picture." She walked around Naya's desk to stay behind her and see it for herself.

Naya right-clicked on the photograph and zoomed in on it.

"See him?"

Naya let out a long, low whistle. "Yeah, I see him. Second from the center in the back row. Caption says he's first baseman Patrick R. McCandless."

"Yep."

Naya turned her gaze to the image on Sasha's cell phone and then back to the photo of the baseball team.

"Holy smokes. They could be twins. Who is this kid?" She waved Sasha's cell phone at her.

Sasha reached for it and pocketed it. "I have no idea, but I guess he's not Karyn and Patrick's kid. I saw him after I dropped Jordana off this morning, and I can't stop thinking about him."

"I can see why. But, no, there's nothing in Karyn Fletcher's background that suggests she has a college-aged kid. The timing works, though, Right?"

Sasha nodded. "Yeah, if Karyn was pregnant when Patrick died, that baby would be nineteen now."

"Maybe she put him up for adoption?" Naya suggested in a tentative tone.

"Maybe so."

There was a long pause. Sasha tried not to shiver as a blast of cold air whooshed through the window and hit the back of her neck.

"What are you going to do?"

"I guess I'm going to go see Karyn and ask her."

Naya opened her mouth as if she were going to argue against that plan, but something about Sasha's expression must have made her change her mind. She clamped her mouth shut and nodded.

After a moment she said, "Let me know if you want company."

"I appreciate it, but I think this is something I need to do on my own. Thanks for finding her." She knew her voice sounded unnaturally tight, but she couldn't manage a more casual tone.

"Sure thing. You sure you're okay?"

She didn't trust herself to speak, so she nodded and bolted from the office. She ran directly into Will Volmer, who was on his way into Naya's office.

"Oops," he said as he reached out an arm to brace her.

"Sorry."

"Not a problem. I'm just heading in for a chat with Naya. She says hiring more junior associates has become an urgent need. Care to join us?"

"Um ... hmm ... uh," Sasha stalled. She was usually adept at avoiding administrative meetings, but her brain was too tired to come up with an excuse. Or form an actual sentence.

He gave her a close look. "Is everything okay? I understand Jordana's gotten herself into a bit of misadventure."

"What? Oh, right. Yes, I don't think the police are going to press charges against her. So, once she catches up on her sleep, she'll be fine. But we did get a new client out of the protest."

"Really?" He turned, his hand on Naya's door.

"He's a professor. I spoke to a witness who says nine men, including Professor Robinson, were abducted and taken to a detention center of some kind. All the students were subsequently released, but the professor and two others are still being held without charges by a group that hasn't asserted any connection with law enforcement."

Will blinked behind his glasses. "Vigilantes?"

"My witness didn't think so. More like ... a secret government agency."

"Yeesh. Are you going to talk to Leo about it?"

She made a noise that could have meant yes and could have meant no. Then she said, "Regardless, I think it's going to involve criminal and constitutional law. Interested in working it with me?"

He grinned. "Absolutely. Pro bono, I assume?"

She shrugged. "The professor's partner made some noises about starting a ComeHelpUs Fund, but I'd rather keep it simple, so probably pro bono."

"Count me in."

"Thanks, Will. I'll fill you in after Naya gives you your marching orders. Do you really want to go into the icebox without a sweater?"

He shot her a wry, knowing grin, then knocked on Naya's door.

13

Charlie gripped the phone so tightly that the molded plastic creaked. *C'mon, c'mon,* he urged silently, *pick up, baby.* Raquel's line rang and rang.

Scott smirked at him. "Maybe she's moved on. You know women."

Charlie ignored him. Her voicemail message began to play in his ear. He depressed the receiver and redialed. He wasn't about to squander his one and only opportunity to speak to Raquel on a recorded message. He'd just keep calling until he got through, and if the old white dude running this place didn't like it, he could pound salt. He couldn't talk to Sam without

Charlie, and he knew it. So he'd have to wait whether he wanted to or not.

"Your buddy Barefoot's getting sprung." Scott tossed off the sentence casually, but he was clearly probing for a reaction from Charlie.

"He's not my buddy, but good for him," Charlie replied as he listened to Raquel's cell phone ring.

"Wonder what he gave the boss in order to get his ticket out of here? Probably something you told him."

"Maybe," Charlie agreed mildly. For all he knew, the guard was lying about Barefoot's release.

Still, he steeled himself for Scott's continued taunting, but before the guard could get his jabs in, Raquel picked up.

"Baby?"

He winced at the raw pain in her voice.

"I'm okay."

"Where are you?"

He wished he knew.

"Some detention facility."

"Not the police station, though, right? Your TA said some vigilantes or something grabbed you up."

"They're not vigilantes." He paused to glance at Scott, whose face was a rock. Blank, hard, giving nothing. "I think they're feds—or federal contractors, most likely."

"Mercenaries?"

Her fear cut through him. "Let's say private military contractors. It sounds nicer, doesn't it?"

"Who gives a crap how it *sounds,* Charlie? What have they done to you?"

"Nothing, really." Yet. "I'm being detained."

"Without charges, by dudes in black outfits, in some secret facility. This is *bad,* stop pretending it isn't. It isn't reassuring; it's infuriating."

That was the point. Raquel had a temper. If she was pissed off, she wouldn't be panicky and anxious.

"Sorry," he said.

He must've sounded as unconvincing as he felt, because Scott rolled his eyes.

"Do you mind giving me a little privacy here?" he hissed.

"Well, yeah, I do mind. Besides, we're recording your call. You don't have any privacy whether I'm here or not," Scott pointed out.

Raquel finished cursing under her breath. "I'm going to kill you when you're safe."

"Sounds counterproductive, really."

That earned him a wry laugh. "They hooked me up with a lawyer for you. Not one from the clinic. She's in private practice. One of your students works for her."

"Who?"

"The lawyer? Uh, let me see, Sasha McCandless-Connelly. That's what I wrote down at least."

"Never heard of her."

"The student's name is Jordana somebody. I didn't catch a last name."

"Morgan."

"What?"

"Jordana Morgan is—never mind, it's not important. Private attorneys are expensive. I don't think—"

"She said they'd do it pro bono. She's done some criminal law, but there's another partner who specializes in it. They'll work on it together. She said they'll file an ... uh, an emergency motion for discovery. She said it's probably a federal case, and the Western District will hear it right away. She said—."

"Tell her not to."

"What?"

"Not yet. Just ask her to wait twenty-four hours."

"Are you joking, Charlie? Your rights are being violated. You're in danger!" Her voice rose, wobbly and screechy.

"Just chill out, baby. Take a breath. I have my reasons."

"Your reasons," she muttered. "Let's hear 'em."

He glanced at Scott. "They're not going to hurt me. I have ... I have something they need, and if I help them—"

She jumped in. "Let me guess. You're protecting someone, aren't you? Another detainee? You know, Charlie, one of these days, your martyr complex is gonna get you killed."

"I'm not being a martyr. And I'm not in that kind of danger."

He didn't think he was, at least. The guy in the suit was intense, but for all the physical posturing, he didn't strike Charlie as a particularly violent guy. Scott and Fox were the muscle. And, yeah, they'd pound him into a pulp without provocation if they were ordered to do it. But they seemed too well trained, too disciplined, to pop off on their own. He'd be okay.

"And they'll release you after you do … whatever it is you're gonna do?"

"I don't know. Maybe," he answered truthfully. Probably not. But if Scott was telling the truth about Barefoot, it was a possibility.

"I don't like this."

"I know, baby. Believe me, neither do I. But just give it one more day. Trust me."

He could hear her huffing while she considered his request. She was fuming, but she'd understand. She always did.

The door creaked open. Fox stuck his head through the doorway and made a slashing motion across his neck. "Time's up. Boss wants to question the mute guy."

"He's deaf. He's not mute," Charlie corrected him. Fox withdrew his head and slammed the door shut.

"What did you say?" Raquel asked.

"Sorry, I wasn't talking to you. I'll see you soon."

"Charlie—"

"I know, be careful."

"No. Be smart."

That's my girl.

He smiled to himself. "I will."

"You freaking better." Her voice was both tender and aggrieved now. A caress and a slap all at once.

Scott reached over and pried the handset from Charlie's hands before Charlie could tell Raquel he loved her. She knew, though. She knew.

"Okay, okay. Let's go." He gave Scott a baleful look and rubbed his wrists, enjoying one last moment of freedom, before he returned his hands to his sides so the guard could cuff them to the waist chain.

He sure hoped he'd read these guys correctly. But he couldn't leave Sam to fend for himself. He straightened his shoulders as much as he could to counter the natural rounding down that the chains caused and lifted his chin, the posture of a warrior walking into battle.

14

K aryn's Mission-style home looked like a movie set. Inviting, charming, homey. Sasha sat in her car and peered across the street at it through a curtain of vibrant red maple leaves and orange and yellow oak leaves. An enormous pile of fallen leaves had been raked into a mound in front of the wide front porch. She envisioned Karyn and her husband swaying gently on the porch swing, sipping coffee, and watching their kids dive into the leaves, breathless with laughter.

This isn't getting you anywhere.

She used the lighted mirror on the underside of the car's sun visor to reapply her lipstick and coax her renegade waves back into the knot of hair at the base of her neck. She looked tired to her own eyes, paler than usual and bleary-eyed. She raised a shoulder and shrugged at her reflection, then snapped the visor up.

She crossed the cobblestone street slowly, listening to the crack and echo of her boots on the stones as she tried to decide on an opening.

Maybe, just maybe, this wasn't the most brilliant idea.

She hadn't intended to come here. Not really. Not yet. She'd run out to get a salad and an omelet for lunch and had somehow ended up in her car, driving north before she'd formed the conscious thought to go see Karyn. But she was here now, so she might as well just push forward.

She followed the brick path to the porch and climbed the stairs. She focused on her breathing as she pressed the doorbell. The chimes sounded inside, and she studied the autumn wreath that hung on the door—pinecones, berries, and swirls of fall-colored leaves. The red berries complemented the tight red chrysanthemum blooms that flanked the door in two stone urns. The effect was elegant, tasteful, polished. A contrast to the wreath that still hung on her own front door, leftover from Halloween. A garish explosion of purple, black, and orange, complete with googly eyeballs and blinking lights. It was Finn's favorite Halloween decoration, and she'd been dragging her feet about taking it down because his delight at the sight of it was infectious.

The white and blue patterned curtain over the glass in the door parted, and Karyn peeked out through the folds in the fabric. Confusion filled her face, and she opened the door partway.

"Can I help you?" Her voice was polite, impersonal, a bit cautious.

Karyn didn't recognize her. But then, why would she? She wasn't sure she'd have known who Karyn was if she'd been in line behind her at the grocery store or had run into her at the park. The Karyn she remembered was boisterous, loud, lively. A fitting foil for Patrick. She used to wear her brassy blonde hair long and high and permed. She'd emphasized her blue eyes with multiple coats of green mascara and heavy purple eyeshadow. She'd had a big, contagious laugh and frenetic energy, always dancing, bouncing, bubbling over with joy—and occasionally anger.

This Karyn was subdued. Pretty in an understated way. Her hair had returned to what Sasha assumed was its natural hue—a dark, ashy blonde—and fell in a sleek bob that grazed her chin. Her bright blue eyes were the same as Sasha remembered, although Karyn's makeup, if any, had been applied with a light, restrained hand.

Sasha smiled and stepped forward. "Karyn, it's been a long time. You look great."

Karyn squinted at her. "Sasha McCandless?" She sounded unsure and maybe a bit hopeful that she was wrong.

"Yep. It's Sasha McCandless-Connelly, now." She extended her hand, and Karyn stared down at it as if she'd never shaken hands before.

"I'm sorry. What ... why are you here?"

She withdrew her hand. "May I come in? Just for a few minutes? Please."

Karyn hesitated and frowned. After a moment, she gave a reluctant nod and stepped back. "Of course."

Sasha followed her into an airy living room, flooded with natural light and decorated in creamy white fabrics. Sasha tried to imagine how long the spotless ivory-colored couch with its plush decorative pillows would last in her home. She gave it a day, tops.

Every surface sparkled. Multiple ceramic vases overflowed with abundant fall bouquets. The room felt peaceful, quiet. Like the woman who studied her from the other side of the hearth.

"Would you like a glass of water? Or I can make tea."

She almost said no. But tea would take a while, give her some time to talk to Karyn. "Tea would be wonderful. Thank you."

"Make yourself comfortable."

Karyn disappeared down a hallway, and Sasha lost her opportunity. She'd hoped to tag along into the kitchen, but she hadn't been invited and she didn't dare push her luck. The conversation she hoped to have was going to be delicate enough. There was no need to upset her hostess before she even got started.

She circled the room, studying the silver-framed family portraits. The Fletcher family smiled back at her from a lakeside picnic, the top of a beach dune, and in front of a Broadway theater. She was about to move onto the books on the bookshelves, when Karyn reappeared carrying a light blue ceramic tray laden with a tea set and a plate of cookies. She rested it on the glass-topped coffee table and gestured for Sasha to take a seat.

She skirted the white couch and chose one of the chevron-patterned armchairs in front of the fireplace. Karyn moved the tea tray to an end table between the chairs and claimed the other.

"So what's this about? Are your parents okay?" Karyn asked as she poured tea into two dainty cups, then glanced at a glass and crystal clock on the mantel piece. "I need to leave to pick the kids up from school in less than an hour."

"I won't be long," Sasha promised. "And my parents are fine. How are you?"

"Sasha, no offense, but I don't think you tracked me down after all this time to see how I'm doing. What do you want?" Her tone was mild. She stirred cream and sugar into her tea and waited for an answer.

"I guess you're on my mind because today's the ..." She trailed off and took a breath and a sip of her tea.

"The twentieth anniversary of Patrick's death." Karyn lowered her gaze and traced a circle around her saucer with one light pink polished fingernail. When she looked back up, there was a shadow in her eyes. "It's understandable that he's on your mind."

"I guess. It's been such a long time since I've seen you."

"At least fifteen years, I'd guess. It just was easier to drift away after a while."

"I understand. It looks like you're happy."

Karyn brightened. "I have a good life. I love my husband; I love my kids. What about you? I've seen you in the papers and on the news. You're some kind of big-time lawyer, right?"

Sasha shook her head. "I'm a lawyer, yeah. And I have a propensity for getting into trouble, so sometimes I'm in the press."

"You always were a firecracker." Karyn grinned at some memory.

"Don't worry, as my mom says, I'm paying for it now. My husband and I have twins. Finn and Fiona turned four over the summer."

She turned her phone toward Karyn to show off her lock screen picture. Karyn took it and glanced at it politely. "I can see the McCandless genes in both of them. Adorable." She tilted her head. "Is your husband Asian?"

"He's Vietnamese-Irish-American. So our

kids are Vietnamese-Irish-Russian-Americans. You know, Heinz 57 varieties."

She cracked the well-worn joke in an effort to make Karyn laugh, but Karyn just smiled. Then she placed the phone on the table between them and gestured to the row of silver-framed photographs. "Britt, Brianna, and Brad don't look anything alike. Although, that's no surprise."

Sasha gave her a quizzical look. "Oh?"

"Well, two of the kids are adopted from two different birth moms with different fathers, and the youngest was the product of assisted reproduction. My husband's sperm, a donor's egg, and a gestational surrogate. So they don't share any genetic material with one another. Or me."

"Oh."

Karyn eyed her.

"Um ... it's funny that you brought up adoption." Sasha winced at the awkward segue.

"Why is that?"

"Because I was wondering if ... maybe ... if there was any chance that you might have been pregnant when Patrick died?" She finished lamely, then sat there feeling like an oaf. The segue had been the least offensive part. She

138 MELISSA F. MILLER

should have planned out what she was going to say.

"Excuse me?"

"I thought maybe you were pregnant when he was killed and decided to put the baby up for adoption, which I would totally understand."

She watched Karyn's face closely as she said the words. She'd expected to see surprise or grief if her hunch was right and confusion or indignation if it was wrong. But what she saw was feral anger, visceral and fierce. It blazed across Karyn's perfectly made-up face. She smoothed it away fast, but Sasha saw it.

And it pricked some long-forgotten memory. Something about Christmas. Before she could probe her mind and shake it loose, Karyn snapped out an answer.

"No, I was not pregnant when Patrick died. And I've never put a child up for adoption. In case you're wondering, I've also never had an abortion. As you may have gathered, I'm infertile." She squared her jaw and stared hard at Sasha.

"I'm so sorry. I know that was a rude question."

"Yes. It was."

"There is no excuse for my behavior. But something happened today." She picked up her phone and swiped back to the picture she'd taken in front of the library. "I saw this boy today. And he's the spitting image of Patrick." She handed the phone to Karyn who took it reluctantly, as if it might burn her or her shock her.

Her lower lip trembled as she studied the picture. Her eyebrows tented in the middle of her forehead and her eyes softened. Then she swallowed and shook her head. "I guess there's a resemblance. But your mind's playing tricks on you, Sasha. Patrick's top of mind because of what day it is, that's all." Her voice was suddenly gentle.

"Maybe, or maybe ..."

She trailed off and watched a long-haired fluffball of a cat—white like the furniture—prowl across the room and wrap itself around Karyn's ankles.

Karyn leaned down and stroked the cat's head absently. "I know you and Patrick weren't particularly close growing up. The oldest and youngest, there was a big age difference, some personality differences. But I also knew you guys started to get closer once you left for college. He loved you and was proud of you. Hang on to that. Remember that."

Sasha's chest tightened, and her face warmed. She nodded, unsure whether she could speak without crying. Karyn seemed to understand, all of her anger had dissipated. But that's how she'd always been. Patrick used to say her temper was hot but short-lived.

Karyn stood, so Sasha did, too. Karyn started moving toward the front hall. The unspoken message was unmistakable. It was time to go. Sasha fell into step beside her.

When they reached the door, Sasha drew a deep breath and said, "I'm truly sorry for upsetting you. I had no right."

As she opened the door, Karyn nodded. "I understand. But, please, listen to me—stop poking around and reopening old sores. You need to leave the past alone."

Sasha stepped out onto the front porch, then turned to respond. But the door was already closed. On the other side, she heard the snick of the deadbolt sliding into place as Karyn locked her out.

15

Christmas Eve, 1999

It was the night before Christmas, and nobody in the McCandless household was feeling particularly festive. Patrick had been dead for five weeks, and the fact of his death hung heavy over the house.

Sasha's dad had insisted they get a tree when she returned from campus for the winter break. Her mom had begged off, but the rest of them—Dad, Ryan and Sean and their wives, and Sasha—had dutifully tromped off into the snow. They'd picked out the first reasonably attractive tree on the makeshift tree lot in the grocery store parking lot without the usual debate.

They made it as far as putting it up in the dining room, where it sat unadorned and somber for weeks. One afternoon, while her parents were out, she'd hauled the bins of ornaments and lights down from the attic. But then she'd stood and stared at the naked tree, trying to summon the energy to decorate it.

She was still standing there when her parents returned.

"Just leave them. I'll get to it," her mom had said.

But she hadn't. Just as she hadn't gotten around to her holiday baking or her shopping or anything, really. Eventually, her dad dragged the boxes into the hall closet so he'd quit tripping over them.

Sasha spent her nights laying awake and listening to her mother cry through the thin shared wall between her bedroom and her parents' room.

She spent her days cocooned in her room, buried under blankets, napping and listlessly watching whatever happened to be on television, until her father came in and dragged her down to a dinner nobody bothered to eat.

Every day seemed grayer, colder, and darker than the last. She couldn't wait for the month, the year, the millennium, to end. Maybe the year 2000 would provide a clear demarcation between a painful past and a fresh future. Maybe the frozen grief that encased them would begin to thaw in the new year.

It was something to hope for, at least.

On Christmas Eve, Valentina McCandless applied her makeup for the first time in a month, sprayed herself with her signature perfume, and announced to her family that they were attending midnight Mass, and Karyn was joining them. Nobody dared argue.

At some point, Karyn arrived. She sat silently in the living room, dressed for church but pale and tired-looking, and stared into the dark dining room at the outline of the naked tree while the rest of them got ready.

They were pulling on their boots and coats to leave, when Mrs. Goldsmith, from next door, rang the doorbell. Sasha's Dad answered it and invited her in from the cold.

"No, no, I know you folks have your

Catholic service coming up. Clive and I just got home from our Christmas Eve service. We Lutherans are early to bed, early to rise, you know."

Dad laughed politely, but Sasha caught him rolling his eyes at her mom.

"Okay, then. Is there something I can do for you? Because you're right, we are just about to leave for church."

"The mail carrier left this on our porch yesterday, but it's addressed to you. You know, Bill is on vacation this week. The fill-in must've gotten the addresses mixed up. Clive was supposed to bring it by yesterday, but he forgot in all the holiday hustle and bustle." She thrust a large box into Sasha's dad's arms and then reached into her oversized handbag.

As soon as she pulled out the foil-wrapped loaf, Sean and Ryan groaned. Riley giggled. Her mom shot them a death glare and stepped forward.

"Daisy, you made your fruitcake," she enthused.

"I know how you all love it," Mrs. Goldsmith beamed.

"It's very kind of you. I'm embarrassed to say

I didn't get my holiday baking done. No nutmeg logs or teacakes from me this year, I'm afraid."

Mrs. Goldsmith patted her arm. "Valentina, dear, go easy on yourself. Such a terrible time of year to lose a child—"

Sasha's mom made a thin whimpering sound. Her dad sprang into action.

"Thank you, Daisy. For delivering our package and for your delicious fruitcake, but we really do need to head out." Sasha's dad stepped forward and herded her onto the porch with an apologetic smile.

"Merry Christmas!" Mrs. Goldsmith called as the door swung shut.

"Who's the gift from, Dad?" Sean asked.

"Um, let's see the return address ... oh, it's from Sasha's roommate. That's sweet."

"Allie?" Jordan asked, her voice unnaturally high.

Sasha turned to her, puzzled. Jordan shook her head.

Sasha's dad sliced through the tape.

Her mom peered inside. "My word," she breathed.

She reached inside and lifted out a porcelain donkey. It was glossy and tan with a gilt-edged saddle and reigns and lifelike blue eyes. She turned it, and it caught the light.

Sasha craned her neck to see what else was in the box, and her dad tilted it, holding it at an angle to display a manger, shepherds, sheep, wise men, Mary, Joseph, and the swaddled baby Jesus. Each piece was more delicate and detailed than the last. A shimmering crystal Star of Bethlehem sparkled above it all. It was opulent, over-the-top, and, Sasha knew, likely cost more than all the furniture in the room, if not the house.

Her mom plucked a sheet of ivory stationery from the box and read aloud:

Dear McCandless Family,

I can only imagine how you're feeling this Christmas. I feel your loss all the way in California. Please know you're all in my thoughts and prayers every day, and so is Patrick, may he Rest In Peace. I hope this Nativity set reminds you of the eternal love and life that a wee infant boy will grant us all.

Joy to the World, Peace on Earth, and Much Love,
   Allie

Jordan and Riley were murmuring to one another. Sasha was just about to ask them what their deal was when Karyn popped to her feet and crossed the room in a blur. Her eyes blazed hot. She grabbed the box right out of Sasha's Dad's arms with shaking hands and flung it against the fireplace. Smashed shards of porcelain rained down on the floor, where they broke into even smaller jagged pieces and scattered.

Sean shouted something that Sasha couldn't make out over Karyn's howling.

"Karyn!" Sasha had to scream to make herself heard.

Karyn wheeled around and glared at her, then grabbed her coat and raced out the front door, slamming it so hard that the pictures shook in their frames and the crucifix banged against the wall.

The rest of them stood in stunned silence for a long moment. Then Sasha's mom took off her coat and went to the utility closet to get the broom and dustpan. Sasha found a trash bag. They cleared the rubble, then Ryan ran the vacuum over the floor to get the smallest slivers.

By the time they'd finished cleaning up the mess, it was after midnight.

Sasha spotted the little donkey peeking out from under the couch. She pulled it out and examined it. Unbroken, it was all that remained of Allie's gift.

"Merry Christmas," she whispered to the figurine. She placed it on the mantel and trudged upstairs to bed.

"Sasha? Hey, Sasha," Leo waved his hand in front of his wife's unfocused eyes.

After a moment, she blinked and snapped to the present from ... wherever she'd been.

"Oh, sorry. How long have you been standing there?"

"Only a minute or two," he lied. He'd been hovering in the doorway to her office for a solid five minutes, waiting to see when she'd notice his presence. The fact that she hadn't was troubling from a situational awareness standpoint, not to mention a concern about the mental health of the woman he loved standpoint.

"Lost in thought."

"Evidently. Thinking about your brother?" He entered the office and pulled the door closed behind him. McCandless, Volmer & Andrews had an open-door policy at work, but sometimes exceptions were called for: like, say, the twentieth anniversary of one's brother's shooting death.

"No. I was thinking about Christmas, actually."

He cocked his head. "That's what happens when you start listening to holiday music the day after Halloween."

"Fair enough." She gave him a small smile. "What are you doing here, anyway? Did I forget a lunch date?"

He glanced at his watch. It was nearly four-thirty.

"That'd be a late lunch. No, Riley called this afternoon to see if the kids wanted to have a cousin playdate. Of course they did. I just dropped them off a couple hours ago."

"*All* the cousins?"

"All the cousins," he confirmed. Riley had been an elementary school teacher before she'd had her own kids. She seemed to miss the chaos of children running around underfoot, and she and Ryan were forever inviting the twins and Sean and Jordan's kids over to play in the enormous fenced yard.

"Nice."

"Yeah." He cleared his throat. "She said she and Jordan went to church with your mom today. Lit a candle for Patrick."

Her eyes drifted to the stack of papers at her elbow. "Mmm-hmm."

"Sasha—"

"I have work to do, Connelly."

He braced his arms on her desk and locked eyes with her. "Denial is not a long-term strategy."

"It's worked for two decades," she shot back.

He sighed. "I stopped by my office and did some digging. I may have something for you on the black van."

Her face softened, but he continued before she could speak. "I'll give it to you, but there's a catch. We're going to a bonfire at Riley and Ryan's tonight. They're ordering pizzas and will rent a movie for the kids. Your parents will be there. Riley said you knew about it—she said it would be like a mini-wake. Tell some stories about your brother, have a few drinks."

The guilt that flickered across her face was confirmation that she did. She knitted her eyebrows together. "It sounds vaguely familiar. I guess it must've slipped my mind."

"But, we'll go?"

She nodded slowly. "Yeah, definitely. I'm looking forward to hearing some Patrick stories."

Something about the way she said it—coupled with how readily she'd agreed—gave him the impression that she was up to something. But she fixed him with a bright, innocent smile.

"Good. I'll tell you about the van later then. I need to run some errands." He'd keep the information as leverage, just in case she had any thoughts of backing out.

"Sure. Sounds good."

She stretched over the desk and kissed him lightly. "I'll finish up here and meet you back at the house."

He nodded, still studying her too-open expression. Yeah, she *definitely* had an agenda. But she'd agreed to go, and that was progress. He'd take it as a win.

"Great. See you in a bit."

The intercom on her phone beeped, and Caroline's voice filled the room. "Sasha, I have a

Raquel Jones on the line for you. I know Leo's in there. Do you want me to put her through?"

Sasha made a shooing motion at Leo. "He's just leaving. Give me a minute to grab my notes and then put her through. Thanks."

Leo waved goodbye and opened the door. When he looked back to see if she wanted the door open or closed for her call, she was already poring over a notebook, her head bent.

He left it ajar and headed down the hall. Whatever was going on with Sasha, he knew one thing for certain: she'd put it aside the minute she had work to do. He just hoped she wouldn't push it away forever.

16

S asha was glad for the interruption. She could tell Connelly wanted to talk to her about Patrick, and she was happy to put off that conversation, even if it meant waiting to find out what he'd learned about the black van.

She pulled out her notes from her earlier conversation with Raquel Jones and hit the button to take the call.

"Ms. Jones? Has something happened since we spoke? The police didn't show up, did they?"

She'd been very clear that if the Milltown Police appeared on her doorstep—with or without a warrant—Raquel was to call her immediately.

"No, I haven't seen any sign of the cops."

Sasha exhaled. "Good."

She hoped the woman wasn't already calling for an update. She'd barely had time to organize her thoughts and fill Will in on the strategy, let alone start drafting an emergency motion. But she also understood the woman's frantic need to do something. Her partner wasn't just missing; he was being held in secret by an unknown group. She found it terrifying; she could only imagine how Raquel felt.

"I heard from Charlie."

Sasha dropped her pen. "You did? He's been released?"

"No. He called me from ... wherever he is. I didn't get any details. He's still in custody."

"Did he say who was holding him? Anything at all?"

"No. Like I said, no details."

"Okay. Well, what *did* he say?"

"I told him about you. I told him you were going to file an emergency motion. He said you should wait a day."

"Wait a day? Ms. Jones—" Sasha started to launch into an explanation as to why that was a terrible idea, but the woman on the other end of the phone cut her off.

"That's what he said."

"Do you understand that an emergency motion won't carry quite so much weight if a judge finds out we sat on it for a whole day?"

"I know. But Charlie asked. He's the client, right?"

"Technically, you're my client. I haven't talked to him. I'd be filing on your behalf to demand your partner's release. A delay will weaken your argument." She kept her tone even and calm despite the fact that she wanted to scream.

"Look, I'm not saying I would do what Charlie's doing. But I have to honor his request."

"I just need you to understand it's going to impact our ability to prosecute this. Do you understand that I'm advising against this?"

There was a long pause. "I do."

She sighed. "It's your call. I'll keep working on it so that it's ready as soon as you and Charlie give me the go-ahead to file."

"Thank you."

"Of course. Is it possible Charlie was ... under duress when he called you?"

"You mean, like being tortured or something?"

That *is* what she meant, she just didn't want

to say it. "Not necessarily. Did you get the sense that he didn't want to say what he was saying?"

She thought for a moment before answering. "Honestly, no. If anything, it seemed like he'd agreed to help them with something and wanted us to wait so he could do it."

"Help them—the men who abducted him at gunpoint?"

Raquel hesitated. Sasha could tell she was trying to work out how to put into words what was probably, at best, a hunch or gut feeling. Sasha trusted those more than the most reasoned analysis.

"Just tell me what happened and how you felt about it. Don't censor or edit yourself. I want to hear what he told you, and what your impressions were. Okay?"

"Okay, sure. He said he needed a little more time. It's seemed like he had some kind of leverage over them. Like he had something they wanted, and if he gave it to them, they'd let him go. He sounded confident and kind of in control. Almost like whatever he was doing was his idea."

Sasha thought for a moment. What kind of leverage could Charlie have that would interest the men holding him?

"Do you think he has information about a crime or another detainee? Maybe he's bargaining?"

"With law enforcement? No way. Charlie wouldn't snitch. And he wouldn't cooperate with an illegal operation. He'd never help them unless …"

"Unless what?"

"Unless he was protecting someone. You heard that student—Troy. He said Charlie stood up for the kids. He's a leader that way. He's quiet, but he does the right thing. If there's somebody else there with him who's vulnerable or being mistreated, Charlie would do anything he could to help them. That I'm sure of."

"Even at his own expense?"

Raquel Jones snorted. "Especially at his own expense. Most of the time when he gets into trouble, that's why. He can't just keep his mouth shut and let stuff go. Not Charlie."

"And you have no idea who he's trying to help or how?"

"I'm not sure, but I thought I heard someone tell him to end the call because it was time to talk to the deaf guy. I might have misheard, though."

Sasha rubbed her forehead. "Assuming you

heard correctly, does that mean anything to you?"

Raquel exhaled loudly. "I could be way off. But Charlie knows sign language. His aunt lost her hearing as a child. He picked it up when he was just a kid so he could talk to his Auntie Rae. He's pretty fluent."

"You think he could be interpreting?"

"Maybe? I mean, yes. If he's being held with someone who's hard of hearing, I think Charlie would offer to sign for him. He sure wouldn't leave him there with no way to communicate." The woman's uncertainty and hesitation melted away, replaced by steel-edged conviction.

"Hmm. I'll see if Rush, Troy, and Jordana had any luck tracking down any of the other students who ended up in the van. Maybe someone noticed a man using sign language."

"Okay. Is there anything I can do to help?"

"Just sit tight. I know it's hard."

"I wish there was something I could *do*."

Raquel sniffled, and Sasha's chest tightened in sympathy.

"I know. Now, I'll be leaving the office shortly. I have an engagement. I will have my cell phone with me. Call or text me at the number I gave you earlier at any time. And I mean *any* time. Call me in the middle of the night. Call me very early in the morning. I don't care what time it is. I need to know what you know when you know it."

"Okay. Thank you. Thank you for doing this for Charlie."

"Of course. Hang in there. We'll get him home to you one way or another."

Her voice broke, and she swallowed a sob. "You call me whenever you want, too. It's not like I'm not going to be sleeping or anything. Not till Charlie's home. He might think he's in control. But guys in black with guns and no one to answer to? That gives me a bad feeling."

You and me both.

"I promise I'll call you right away if I need to talk to you. I do hope you'll try to get some rest. You've spoken to Charlie, and you say he sounds good. He's alive. That's more than we knew just hours ago."

"I guess."

"It's true. Take a walk. Take a nap. Make sure you eat some protein and drink lots of water. You have to take care of yourself, so you can take care of Charlie when we get him out."

If we get him out.

"You're right."

She ended the call and reviewed her notes, flipping her pen against her desk. Charlie Robinson might think that he could outsmart or work with or do whatever it was he thought he was doing with whomever these people were. But she didn't like it. Her eyes fell on the notes from the interview with Troy. She'd circled the name Barefoot.

She dropped the pen on her desk and turned toward the computer screen. She opened the Allegheny criminal records database and typed in 'Barefoot.'

Bingo. With a few keystrokes, she had his name, record, and address.

What she planned to do with this information, she had no idea. But a visit to Mr. Barefoot was probably in order.

She checked the time. Not tonight.

She'd promised to go to the bonfire, and she didn't want to get into a whole thing with Connelly. He thought she sometimes used work as an excuse to avoid dealing with personal issues. Even after all this time, he didn't seem to understand that her client's needs were often urgent, important, and demanded immediate attention. Her issues, such as they were, stemming from her brother's death or whatever, could be dealt with at any time. It's not like they were going anywhere.

But this time, she had reasons of her own for wanting to see her brothers and their wives.

She stood up and pushed back her chair. She'd update Will on the call from their client and then head out. Mr. Barefoot would keep until the morning.

17

O fficer Scott shoved Charlie Robinson into the room, not as roughly as the last time. This time the man stayed on his feet.

Landon studied Robinson's face. He needed to get a read on him before he started questioning Sam Blank.

"Did you make your phone call?"

"Yes. Thanks." Robinson glanced around the room.

"What?"

"Nothing. I was just hoping you'd have some more chairs brought in."

"Ah, missing the creature comforts are you, professor?"

The man gave him a lopsided smile. "Not exactly."

Landon drew himself up straight. "Perhaps you can post a review of your stay on one of the hospitality industry sites after you leave us."

Officer Scott snickered.

The prisoner shook his head. "Makes no difference to me, man. But if you want me and Sam to sign, we'll need our hands. I thought you might feel better if our legs were cuffed to some chairs. Aren't you scared we might, I don't know, hobble over to you and choke you to death?"

Officer Scott sprang forward and pushed Charlie Robinson against the rough stone wall. "Is that supposed to be a threat?" He snarled.

"It's an observation."

The guard cut his eyes toward Landon, who clicked his tongue against his teeth. "The professor's right. I hadn't considered the issue of the prisoners having their hands free. Please scare up two more chairs. We'll do just as he suggests and shackle them to the chair legs."

Scott opened his mouth as if he might protest, and Landon silenced him with a look.

He released his grip on Robinson's shirt and nodded. "Yes, sir."

"Thank you. And tell Officer Fox to bring the other prisoner while you're at it."

Scott left, and Landon studied Charlie Robinson.

"What?" Robinson demanded.

"I beg your pardon?"

"You obviously want to ask me something. I can't imagine what's stopping you. Ask away."

Landon shook his head. "You misunderstand. I don't have any questions for you, Mr. Robinson. I'm trying to determine if I can trust you to interpret faithfully."

Robinson took his time answering. "Don't suppose you have much choice." He tried to shrug. The motion of his shoulders was hampered by the handcuffs attached to his waist chain.

"No, I don't suppose I do." Landon leaned forward, intent on restoring the balance of power. "I may need you now. But don't mistake expediency for weakness. I'll be video recording this interview so it can be reviewed in the future if need be. If I find out you're doing anything other than signing exactly what I ask and relaying Mr. Blank's responses verbatim, you'll regret it. That's neither a threat nor an observation, by the way. It's a promise." He flashed a tight smile.

Robinson was studying him. "You have access to an interpreter? Then why don't you just call him or her in to handle the interview?"

"As I may have mentioned earlier, it will take some time for me to locate and vet an American Sign Language expert. I'm using you for convenience, that's all. But I'll certainly be able to have your interpretation checked," he said blandly.

"Sure thing. By an ASL expert, right?"

"That's what I said."

Robinson pushed out his lower lip and nodded, as if the answer satisfied him.

Landon would have pushed the issue further, but just then there was a loud rap on the door. He pushed the buzzer to unlock it, and Scott came into the room trailed by Fox and the prisoner.

Scott carried a pair of heavy metal chairs one-handed, his massive arm bulging under his tight black base layer. Fox was prodding a middle-aged Black man into the room.

Sam Blank glanced at Charlie Robinson, then turned to Landon. His hazel eyes were flat and hard. Familiar. Landon's pulse ticked up.

. . .

It was 2009. Calvin Tennyson's lifeless hazel eyes stared up at him. Cold and unseeing.

Calvin James Tennyson had been cutting through the park, his head bent and hands jammed into his jacket pockets. The patrol officer who stopped him later said he seemed calm. In a hurry, but polite and helpful. He assured the officer that he didn't know anything about any dead boy bleeding out in the alley, hadn't heard any gunshots, nothing like that. The officer—relying on instinct, his gut, nothing more tangible than a feeling—checked his ID, took down his name and address, and sent him on his way.

By the time a witness came forward and placed Tennyson at the scene, Josh had been dead for three months and Calvin Tennyson was in the wind. A career criminal with two strikes, he'd talked his way out of the stop in the park, then vanished.

That first year—after Josh—he'd focused on finding Tennyson, tracking down the man who killed his son. In the early days, that had been his mission. But then Tennyson's body was found in North Carolina, in a small town where he had family. Like Josh, he fell victim to a violent crime. Stabbed, not shot. In a tidy, wood-paneled den, not a grimy alley. The investigating officers told Landon they had no leads, and Tennyson's death wasn't a priority. One of them gave him a crime scene photograph, a closeup of Calvin's Tennyson's face, his sightless eyes. It was all the closure he would get.

After Tennyson's murder, Landon needed a new quest to give his grim existence meaning. That's when he dreamed up Cesare, when he'd set his sights on helping all the Joshes, all their families.

With two prior felonies in his background, if Tennyson had been arrested, charged and convicted for Josh's murder, he would have served a life sentence. But what if someone had predicted his future crime and taken him off the street before he'd committed another crime? The idea haunted Landon.

OFFICER FOX CLEARED HIS THROAT. Landon pulled his gaze away from Sam Blank's eyes and shook himself back to the present. Officer Scott was still holding the chairs and waiting for instruction.

"Set those down so they'll be clearly visible on the video." He waved at the camera on the tripod behind him.

"You want video, sir?" Fox didn't hide his surprise.

"Yes, I'll be recording this session in case I need to have the sign language translation verified."

It was a highly unusual move. The three windowless basement rooms were set aside for when particularly vigorous and muscular forms of interrogation were employed. But he needed a way to keep Robinson in line and to ensure he didn't coach the witness.

"We could've just done this in a regular room," Scott mumbled.

Landon ignored him.

Scott thumped down the chairs on the ground, and he and Fox pushed the prisoners into the seats. They fastened their ankle restraints to the chair legs, then freed their hands. Both men rubbed their wrists and shook out their hands.

Landon jerked his chin toward the door, dismissing the guards. They left, and he crossed the room and slid the iron bar into place across the door. He turned on the video recorder and clapped his hands together.

"Let's get started."

18

Charlie caught Sam's eyes as they settled into the chairs. He flashed a *'B'* under the guise of massaging his wrists. Sam didn't react other than to blink, but Charlie figured he understood.

They would use BSL instead of ASL to communicate. Most people had no idea that Black Sign Language and American Sign Language were two distinct languages. Charlie hadn't known until college.

He learned BSL to talk to his Aunt Rae, and he was pretty adept. So, in college, he chose ASL to fulfill his foreign language requirement, thinking it would be an easy A. On the first day of class, he realized his error. It was the equiva-

lent of thinking you can speak Spanish just because you speak Italian. They were both Romance languages, but they were two completely different Romance languages. On his first trip back home, he'd peppered Aunt Rae with questions. Turns out, BSL had originated in the Deep South, in segregated schools for the deaf and, like so many aspects of culture, it had spread. Now Charlie could code-switch between the two sign languages just as he code-switched between AAE and SAE, speak one way with certain folk and another way with others.

By using BSL, he and Sam would have some measure of privacy, even under the watchful eye of the video recorder. Sure, this guy might eventually learn that they hadn't been signing in ASL, but that would take time. And he'd need to find a BSL interpreter willing to work for ... whatever this outfit was. Using their own dialect wasn't going to solve all their problems, but it was something.

The questioner cleared his throat. "Let's get started. State your name and address for the record."

Charlie signed the question. Sam answered.
```
```

"My name is Samuel Lawrence Blank, and I don't have an address."

"You're homeless?"

Sam shrugged, then signed, "At the moment."

Charlie signed back that his place was a one-bedroom apartment, but he had a futon in the living room, and Sam was welcome to it.

"I didn't ask a question. What did you just say to him?"

"I told him he could sleep on my couch if he needed a place to stay—when we get out of here."

"Limit yourself to the questions I ask and the answers he gives."

"Will do," Charlie lied smoothly.

The man asked Sam about his warrant. Sam signed that, about a month ago, he had needed to make water, but the deli and the corner store had both already banned him from using their bathrooms, so he went behind a tree in the park. The spot wasn't visible from the street, but someone must've seen him from the houses up on the hill and called the police.

Charlie's hands stopped moving, and he gaped at the man. "Seriously? He has a warrant for peeing on a tree?"

The man shrugged, unconcerned. "Take it up with the local PD. Let's get back to it."

He moved on to the topic of the night of the protest, and Charlie's heart thumped in his chest. They needed to be careful here. The less Sam said about Vaughn Tabor, the better.

"Why did you go to the protest?" The man demanded.

"Why were you at the protest that night? What do you want me to tell him?" Charlie clarified.

Sam paused, then he signed, "Does he know?"

"Does he know you saw Vaughn die? I don't think so."

"I heard about the boy's death and wanted to pay my respects. Tell him I thought there might be food there. Sometimes at vigils, the protestors have snacks."

Good, Charlie thought. *Believable story, not easily disproved.* He passed the response along, while Sam nodded in enthusiastic agreement.

"Snacks," the man muttered to himself.

He looked from Charlie to Sam and then back to Charlie, then he leaned forward and rested his elbows on his thighs. "Okay, look. I'm gonna be straight with you. I don't know why the Milltown police are interested in this man. My AI program doesn't clear it up. Maybe Mr. Blank can tell me, because, frankly, I don't understand why he's here. It can't be because he took a leak against a tree."

Charlie sat back. He hadn't expected this guy to place his cards on the table, but he didn't get the feeling the man was bluffing.

He signed the question for Sam, who frowned and started signing more animatedly.

"I've been on the wrong side of the Milltown cops for years. They don't like it when I fall asleep on the benches. They kick me awake and tell me to move on. They don't like it when I sit in front of stores and restaurants. In the winter, they tell me to leave the library. I think, when they saw me at the protest, it just made them mad."

The man frowned.

"Can I ask you a question?" Charlie didn't wait for his agreement. "Your guys showed up before the Milltown police. So they didn't target him, you and your racist computer program did. I mean, right?"

The man's nostrils flared. Charlie didn't really expect an answer, but he got one.

"Again, Cesare is an artificial intelligence application. It can't be racist or not racist. We used the traffic camera at the intersection to scan the protest for persons of interest. Those of you who were hits were gathered up in the van. Everyone except Mr. Blank, that is. Cesare didn't flag him. The Milltown police asked me to add him to the list. They've declined to share their reasoning, and, frankly, having talked to him, I'm inclined to release him. I don't like being used."

Charlie blinked. "I'm glad to hear that, and I'm sure Sam is, too. I understand you've also released Mr. Barefoot." He left the rest unsaid.

The man tented his fingers together. "And you want to know if you can go, too. Yes, I'm prepared to release you both. Of course, you'll both need to sign the same nondisclosure agreement and liability waivers that Mr. Barefoot signed."

"Yeah, sure. Whatever you need." He didn't care what he had to sign to get out of there. He was going home, and that's all that mattered.

19

R yan and Sean were in the backyard building the bonfire when Sasha and Connelly arrived. He beelined through the house to join her brothers as they poked at logs and did whatever other tasks stoking a bonfire entailed.

Sasha wandered into the kitchen and hugged her sisters-in-law.

"Where are the kids?"

Riley was plating cheese and crackers with a glass of red wine in one hand. She gestured with her glass toward the basement door. "They're down there watching a movie. Liam's in charge."

Jordan maneuvered around Riley's kitchen as

if it were her own. She reached over Riley's head and pull down a wineglass for Sasha. "Drink?"

"Yes, thanks."

Jordan poured out a glug of wine and handed her the glass. She perched on one of the barstools that lined the kitchen island.

"Do you need any help?" Sasha asked, even though she could count on one hand the times that either of her brothers' wives had taken her up on an offer to lend a hand in the kitchen. She wasn't exactly known for her command of the domestic arts.

"You just sit there and look pretty," Riley grinned.

She sipped her wine. "Now that I can do. I'm glad you decided to do this tonight."

Jordan slid her a sidelong glance. "Are you?"

Riley shifted her attention from the cheese she was cubing to Sasha's face to see her answer.

"Of course. Why wouldn't I be?"

She addressed Jordan, but Riley answered, "The guys thought you might not want to do the whole remembering Patrick thing. You've always been sort of ... funny about it."

She felt her right eyebrow inching toward

her hairline and struggled to keep her expression neutral. "Funny, how?"

Riley focused on filling a glazed ceramic bowl with olives while she responded. "You know, you never want to go to church and light a candle with your mom. And half the time you're late for Thanksgiving dinner—if you even come."

"Whoa, whoa. Hang on. I think I've missed two Thanksgiving dinners over the past twenty years, and both times it was because I had to—"

"Work," they said in unison.

She caught her lip between her teeth. The inflection in their voices left no question what they thought about her career.

"Listen, if I wanna have an argument about work-life balance, I'll wait till my mom gets here. Can't we just drink our wine and enjoy the soundproof basement?"

Her attempt at levity worked.

Riley chuckled. "Sure."

Jordan clinked her glass against Sasha's. "Here's to finished basements."

The tension in the kitchen dissipated, and they sat in companionable silence for a while.

The only sound was Riley's knife hitting the cutting board.

After a moment, Riley said, "Speaking of Thanksgiving, just so you know, Daniella has decided she's a vegan."

"Oh? Does that mean Valentina will be making a Tofurkey?" Jordan wondered.

Sasha nearly did a red wine spit-take all over Riley's spotless center island. "Could you imagine?" She gasped, trying not to laugh.

They were still giggling when Connelly came in to grab some beers from the refrigerator.

"Fire's coming along nicely," he informed them. He stopped to drop a kiss on the crown of Sasha's head. He smelled of smoke and fresh air.

"Great. We'll bring out some snacks in a minute. I'll wait until Val and Pat get here to order the pizza," Riley answered.

"Sounds good."

Sasha waited until he stepped out onto the deck and shut the sliding door behind him. Then she said, "Thanksgiving's next week. Before we know it, it'll be Christmas."

"Mmm-hmm," Jordan said absently.

"Remember the first Christmas after Patrick died? You were there when Karyn smashed up that nativity set my college roommate sent to Mom and Dad, right?"

Jordan and Riley exchanged a long look, but neither spoke.

"What?" She demanded.

Jordan let out a long, slow breath. "Yeah, I remember."

"It's kind of hard to forget," Riley added in a quiet voice.

Her sisters-in-law shared yet another meaningful look.

She tried again. "I always wondered why she did that. I know she was probably in a bad place —we all were—the first Christmas without Patrick. But it was so out of character. So strange, really."

Riley rested the knife on the cutting board and leveled her gaze at Sasha. "I don't think Karyn was acting strangely at all. Considering ..."

"Riley," Jordan warned.

"Really? She destroyed a gift, an expensive, thoughtful one, for no reason," Sasha countered.

"Oh, she had her reasons," Riley responded.

Jordan shook her head, grabbed the wine bottle, and refilled all three glasses. "You're gonna need it," she muttered under her breath as she handed Sasha her glass.

"I don't think Karyn cared about the cost of the gift, Sasha, because your roommate slept with her husband."

What?!

Sasha sucked in her breath. She was quiet for a long moment while she processed—or tried to, anyway—Riley's claim. Finally, she shook her head.

"No. There's no way. I don't know what Karyn *thought* happened between Allie and Patrick, but there is *no way* my roommate had an affair with my brother. He was married. He was ten years older than her, for crying out loud. Just ... no."

Riley sighed and looked at Jordan as if to say *'your turn.'*

Jordan smiled sadly. "Do you remember that cloying body lotion Allie used to wear?"

"That pear stuff? Sure. How could I forget? Our entire dorm room reeked of it," Sasha laughed.

"Yeah, well, the summer before Patrick died, when she stayed with you while her parents were in Europe, Karyn said Patrick would come home from your parents' place with the scent clinging to him."

"So? That doesn't mean they were having an affair."

"You didn't think it was weird how upset she was at Patrick's funeral?" Riley prodded.

"Of course, she was upset. She was like a member of the family. But she wouldn't betray our friendship by sleeping with Patrick. Besides, he would never cheat on Karyn."

"They were going through a rough patch, Sasha," Riley said in a low voice. "They were having trouble getting pregnant. It was causing a lot of stress. She wanted to try for IVF, but they couldn't afford it. He was working a lot of hours to make extra money. They were fighting ... things were bad. And then Allie came along. Rich, pretty, young, and starry-eyed. She thought he was amazing, and he lapped up the attention."

"No!" Sasha slapped her hand down on the top of the island. "You're wrong. I'm going to go check on the kids."

She shook with anger as she crossed the room and yanked open the basement door.

Behind her, Jordan said, "He told Sean, Sasha. I'm sorry, but it happened."

Sasha raced down the stairs without responding. Even as her brain refused to believe the words, the truth was cracking her heart wide open.

20

B y the time Landon finished recording his observations and updating Cesare's database, it was after six. He sped from the facility over to the Milltown Police Department in a desperate bid to catch the chief of police before he left for dinner.

Even as he peeled around the corner and careened into the parking lot, he knew he was too late. The chief's distinctive burnt-orange Hummer wasn't in the lot. He should've called instead, but old habits dictated that he have as many conversations about the program face-to-face as possible. After all, he of all people knew there was always somebody listening to one's phone calls.

He jerked the wheel and hit the brakes, squealing to a stop in the first empty space. As he killed the engine, he scanned the lot. Kara Diamond's subcompact was in her usual spot. She wasn't the chief, but she was nearly as good.

His mood lightened, and he strode quickly into the building.

"Hello," he boomed, startling the officer at the front desk—a fresh-faced, dark-haired woman whom he didn't recognize. He leaned forward to read her badge. "Officer Comford, I'm here to see Officer Diamond. Tell her it's Landon Lewis."

The officer fidgeted with her duty weapon at her hip. The motion appeared to be a nervous tic, but it was an unfortunate one. It was the kind of mindless habit that could get a law enforcement officer killed. Or indicted.

"Sure thing. Wait right here."

She disappeared into the warren of cubicles and returned a few moments later with Kara in tow.

"Twice in twenty-four hours. It must be my lucky, interminable day," Kara said in greeting.

He laughed and approached the desk to

shake her hand. "I'm surprised to see you still here. Didn't you work midnight to eight yesterday?"

"I wish. No, my shift started at four o'clock yesterday afternoon. I should've clocked out at midnight, same as tonight. But all those girls came in on the bus and it didn't seem ...." She paused and cut she her eyes to the officer stationed at the desk. After a moment, she went on, "... It seemed better to have a female officer present."

That was all she said, but it spoke volumes. The duty officer lowered her eyes and stared at the counter. He assumed the unspoken subtext involved sexual harassment—or worse—of female prisoners. It was not a topic he wanted to have illuminated, in any case.

"Fair enough. I have a report on the protestors who were sent over to the PPC unit."

"The chief left for supper."

"Yeah, I figured, I didn't see his Hummer in the lot. You're still on the task force, though, right? I can fill you in. We can go somewhere and I'll buy you a drinkable cup of coffee. You must be running on fumes at this point."

She twisted her lips to the side and considered the offer. "Thanks, but I can't leave. I'm in charge until the shift change. We'll borrow the chief's office so we'll have some quiet."

"Lead the way."

He trailed her through the maze of desks, holding cells, and interview rooms. In the rear left corner of the building, they reached a large square office with a shade pulled down over the glass door. She tried the handle; it was unlocked.

She opened the door, and he followed her inside. She turned on the light and gestured around. "Have a seat."

He took one of the visitor's chairs in front of the Chief's desk and watched her eye the massive leather seat behind the desk. After a moment, she thought the better of it and claimed the chair next to Landon's.

Observes the hierarchy even when senior officer not present, he noted automatically.

She removed a small spiral notebook and a ballpoint pen from the breast pocket of her uniform shirt, uncapped the pen, and positioned it over the notepad. "You don't mind if I take notes, do you?" She asked the question by rote, with no real interest in his answer.

"I'd rather you didn't, to be honest. But I understand if you want to be sure you report accurately to the chief tomorrow. So I just ask that after you've briefed him face to face, you get rid of any notes."

Her face tightened. "Destroying official documents? I don't know Landon."

"Trust me, it's not destruction of evidence. You're just protecting the top-secret nature of this program."

After a moment, she shrugged. "You're the boss."

"I appreciate your accommodation." He smiled at her. With that out of the way, he plunged into the purpose for his visit. "All nine of the targets who were identified last night have been cleared and released."

"I heard about the students earlier today. Six of them were dropped off at the protest site."

"That's correct," he confirmed.

"And you cleared the other three, too?"

"I personally interviewed and assessed the remaining targets—Mr. Barefoot, Mr. Blank, and Professor Robinson—and made the determination to cut them loose."

"Based on what your program said?" She

looked up from the notes she was writing in neat script.

"Based partially on the artificial intelligence recommendation and partially on my own assessment of their potential latent criminality."

She frowned. "I don't understand the point of your fancy program then. Cesare pinged them as people it predicted would commit crimes, right? So, you just have a chat with them and send them on their way? I don't see the point, Landon. No offense."

He smiled, but there was no warmth behind it. "None taken, Kara. Look, Barefoot will commit another violent crime. I have no doubt. That's why my team has been instructed to set up wire-taps, electronic surveillance, and a ground team to monitor him. When he moves, we'll know. And we'll let you know."

"Good. What about the other two?" Her tension eased somewhat, replaced by a measure of satisfaction.

"Charlie Robinson is, I believe, a paper tiger."

He watched as she doodled a flower in the top corner of the page. "Meaning what?"

"Meaning that he's going to continue to be

involved in protests, agitation, and demonstrations. It's more or less part of his job description to present as politically engaged."

"I don't like that."

"Well, there's a natural check on his behavior. He has to walk a line if he wants to keep his position at the university. So, while Cesare raises concerns about his activism, on balance I believe he'll keep his protesting behaviors on the peaceful, legal side of the line—at least most of the time. Don't worry, my team will keep an eye on the professor, as well. Our monitoring simply won't be as robust as what we put in place for Barefoot."

"I guess that makes sense."

"And that leaves Sam Blank."

"He's the one the chief's most interested in," Kara observed.

Landon found himself leaning forward. "Why is that?"

Kara shrugged. "I'm not sure."

"I'd like to know. Cesare didn't surface any flags on Blank. And my interview showed no evidence that he's committed a serious crime in the past or that he's inclined to commit any future crimes. His inclusion in the group is puzzling."

"I thought Blank had an outstanding warrant?" she mused.

"For pissing against a tree. That's hardly the sort of crime Cesare is designed to predict and prevent. I'm not expending any resources on Blank or setting a team on him. There's no reason to."

Her eyes flashed. "The chief really wants him, Landon."

"There's nothing there, Kara."

She lifted both hands toward the ceiling in frustration. "Willard saw his face on the traffic camera and recognized him. Said he had a warrant. I didn't know it was for public urination."

"Did you know he's deaf? He has a total hearing loss. I had to scramble find an interpreter."

He stared hard at her. She looked back unblinkingly. Then, after a moment, she shifted her gaze to stare down at her little notepad.

"Would've been better for him if he were blind." She said it under her breath, more to herself than to him.

"What's that supposed to mean?"

She shrugged.

He waited, but she just capped her pen and closed up her notebook. "Thanks for the update. I'll be sure to pass it on to Chief Carlson."

21

I t wasn't true. It couldn't be true. The only problem was, she knew it was true.

Patrick had cheated on his wife with her best friend. Her best friend had slept with her brother. Sasha wasn't sure who she was madder at, Allie or Patrick. All she knew for sure was that she'd been betrayed by both of them.

She snuggled up against Connelly and watched the flames dance in the darkness, but she found she couldn't listen to the stories the others were telling. The words crashed against her like waves against rocks. But she wasn't able to absorb them because every story was a new opportunity to probe and pick at the pain that rose in her chest.

Had Allie stayed with her that summer just to get closer to Patrick? Or did it go back even further? Was Patrick the reason she hadn't moved into her sorority house but had asked Sasha to room with her sophomore year? She'd definitely met Patrick when he visited in the spring of her freshman year. She tried to remember when she and Allie had grown close. Was it before or after her brothers' road trip to see her?

Her thoughts continued to unspool:

Had it been Patrick's idea or her idea to try rock climbing together? Was he just trying to weasel his way into Sasha's confidence to gain access to her roommate?

Her mind got stuck on another truth: Patrick had been about to turn thirty, Allie had been a sophomore in college. What had he been thinking? What had she been thinking?

Sasha was spiraling, and the questions were making her sicker and sicker to the point where she really thought she might vomit. She focused on taking deeper, slower breaths and paying closer attention to the moment: the smell of the fire; the crackle of the logs; and the taste of the olive brine lingering on her tongue.

Connelly nudged her shoulder with his. "Did you hear me?"

She shook her head. "No, sorry."

"I said Ryan asked if it's okay if the kids sleep over tonight. Daniella and Julian have an in-service day tomorrow, so it doesn't matter if they stay up late. The teenagers all have school in the morning, but Siobhan and Colin are going to stay anyway. What do you think?"

What she thought was that there was no chance any of them would get any sleep. But she also knew that Finn and Fiona loved sleepovers with their cousins more than almost anything else in the world.

"Sure. I'll run home and get their pajamas and toothbrushes," she offered eagerly. Anything to get out of the rest of the bonfire.

"No need. I had a feeling this is how tonight would end up, so I packed them a bag. They're all set."

Sometimes having the most competent husband in the world was a real pain.

"Great," she said weakly.

He squinted at her in the firelight. "Are you all right?"

"Yeah," she lied. "I'll go get the kids ready for bed."

"I guess it is getting pretty late. I'll help you."

"No, don't be silly. Enjoy the fire. I've got this."

She flashed him a smile and fled the circle.

She herded her sleepy children into the bathroom, washed their saucy faces and sticky hands, and helped them brush their teeth.

As she was easing Fiona's pajama top over her head, Fiona asked in a muffled voice, "Why are the grownups all telling stories about a stranger?"

Sasha smoothed the fleece unicorn pajamas over her daughter's shoulders before answering. "Those are stories about your Uncle Patrick."

Finn frowned and hopped toward her with one leg through his pajama bottoms and one leg out.

"Easy buddy, you're going to trip." She reached out to balance him and help him pull up his pants.

Once he was steady on his feet, he fisted his hands on his hips. "we don't have an Uncle Patrick. We have an Uncle Sean and an Uncle Ryan."

"And an Aunt Riley and an Aunt Jordan," Fiona added.

"And we have an Uncle Friend Hank and an Uncle Friend Chris and Uncle Friend Daniel, but they're not our *real* uncles," Finn informed her.

"Right. Just like Aunt Naya and Aunt Maisy aren't really our aunts. But we don't know anybody called Uncle Patrick." Fiona fixed Sasha with a look she recognized from the mirror.

Heaven help her, she was being deposed by not one, but two, mini-lawyers.

She sank down onto the plush bathmat and tucked her heels under her butt, then pulled Finn and Fiona close, balancing one on each thigh.

"You're right. You don't know your Uncle Patrick. That's because he died before you were born. Patrick was mommy's brother. He was also Uncle Sean's brother and Uncle Ryan's brother."

There was a long silence while they considered this.

"So, Pap Pat and Grandma Val are his mom and dad?" Finn asked, seeking clarification.

"That's right, honey."

Fiona wrinkled her forehead. "When did he die? Did Daddy ever meet him?"

Sasha's heart heaved in her chest. For a moment, she didn't know if she'd be able to get the words out. After a breath, she did.

"No, Daddy never met your Uncle Patrick. He died when I was in college. A long time before I knew your Daddy," she explained.

"Did the cousins know Uncle Patrick?" Fiona asked.

"No. He died even before Liam was born. That's why we're having the bonfire tonight. He died twenty years ago today. So, this is a memory night. It's like a birthday or anniversary, only he's not here."

Finn reached up and stroked her cheek. "That sounds sad, Mommy."

"It is sad. But it's also happy to remember people who died. That way they live on through your memories even though they're gone."

He buried his face in her neck.

"Uncle Patrick doesn't have any kids?" Fiona asked.

Sasha looked at her daughter over her son's head. As she stared into the green eyes that were so like her own, she really couldn't begin to formulate an answer. The answer was no. Right?

And yet, she couldn't shake the image of the student outside the library.

She realized they were waiting for an answer.

"No, no kids." She smoothed Finn's hair and pulled Fiona close for a moment. "Come on, let's get you two snuggled up in your sleeping bags."

After the twins were settled in—or as settled in as they were likely to be in a basement with their six cousins, Sasha passed out hugs and kisses, dimmed the lights, and implored the kids to keep it down to a dull roar. She explained that if the adults could pretend they were sleeping, they could stay awake. But if they made so much noise that someone had to come downstairs and intervene, they would have to go to sleep. The teenagers nodded along sagely as she doled out advice on how to stay just this side of the law.

She climbed the stairs to the kitchen and was digging around in the refrigerator looking for the sparkling water, when her dad appeared in the hallway.

"I didn't know you were in here, Dad."

"Had to hit the head, honey."

"Delightful."

"Hand me one of those bubbly waters, would you?"

She grabbed two at random and passed one to her dad. "I assume you're not fussy about flavor?"

"You assume correctly. What were you doing in the basement?"

"Getting the kids ready for bed—or trying to, at any rate."

Her dad smiled a distant, fond smile. "I remember the sleepovers you four used to have with your pals. Those were some good times."

Her stomach lurched. The last "pal" who'd ever slept at her parents' house had been Allie.

"Mmm-hmm."

"Sasha, are you feeling okay? You're awfully pale, and you've been quiet all night."

She leaned back against the counter and braced herself with her elbows. "Dad, can I tell you something?"

He eyed her cautiously. "Yes?"

He didn't sound too sure, but she needed to tell someone, so she forged ahead. "I want to show you a picture."

"Okay."

She pulled out her phone and swiped open her photo gallery. Once she found the photo of the boy, she enlarged it and passed the phone to her dad.

He squinted at the image for a moment, then moved so that he was positioned directly under the lights shining down on the kitchen sink. He angled the phone and cocked his head.

"Now where would that have been taken? Is that Pat hanging out after baseball practice?"

"I think you know it's not, Dad. I spotted that kid this morning on campus at Chatham."

He handed her back the phone. "Huh."

"Dad, I went to see Karyn today."

His shoulders stiffened, and his face turned stony. "Leave it alone, Sasha."

"Leave what alone?"

"Don't start digging around in the past. You need to let this go."

"Riley and Jordan said—"

"Sasha! Stop. Don't do this." He cut her off sharply.

She stepped back and blinked at him, wide-eyed. She couldn't recall a time when he'd spoken to her with such anger.

He softened his tone. "Tell me you'll let this go. Please."

"I'll let it go," she lied.

22

Leo glanced at his wife as they hurried down the street from Ryan and Riley's home. She'd refused her parents' offer of a lift, saying it was a nice night for a walk. It was a nice, if frosty, night. The sky was clear, the crescent moon was a dim sliver, and the stars were bright and plentiful.

But it wasn't the night air that caused Sasha to turn down the ride. She was brittle and stiff while she said her goodbyes to her parents.

"Finn was already asleep when I went down to tell the kids goodnight," he remarked.

"Hmm. Good for him. I doubt Fiona will sleep a wink."

They walked in silence for a bit. Then he said, "Something happen with your dad?"

She turned her head sharply to stare at him, then laughed softly. "No flies on you. Yeah, we had a bit of a disagreement. Hey, you never told me what you found out about the black van."

It was a change of subject, but a fair one. He had promised to fill her in if she agreed to go to the bonfire, after all.

"They aren't federal agents."

"I'm actually somewhat surprised to hear that."

He'd been surprised, too. The tactics she'd described were straight out of the shadow agency playbook. Not that he'd tell her that.

She tilted her head. "So, what then? Private military contractors?"

"The muscle, maybe. A lot of those guys are independent contractors. Even if they work for a PMC, they freelance on the side. But the program isn't being run by a PMC or a defense contractor or anything like that. Believe it or not, it's a tech company.

"A tech company. Like Silicon Valley?"

"As a matter of fact, yes. Well, originally. A guy named Landon Lewis, who used to work for

PicaPage and then NetworkUp, left the social media sphere to start a company called PPC. It's headquartered in Bakery Square now."

"Just a stone's throw away."

"Yep."

"So, what's that stand for—PPC?"

He raked his fingers through his hair. "That's an excellent question. I don't know. All I know is that PPC isn't officially connected with any of the federal intelligence or law enforcement agencies. But it does receive federal grants to develop tools to be used in predictive and preventive policing."

"Sounds like *Minority Report.*"

"It sort of is," he told her. "But instead of psychics, the 'pre-cogs' in real life are complicated artificial intelligence programs."

"Computers predicting crimes that haven't been committed yet—what could possibly go wrong?" she said drily.

Her reaction was about what he'd expected. "Lewis was inspired to create Cesare because of a tragedy in his personal life," he told her, repeating what he'd learned from a series of off-the-record phone calls with buddies spread throughout the law enforcement community.

"Cesare?"

"That's the name of the AI. Probably named for Cesare Lombroso."

"And who is Cesare Lombroso?"

"He was a criminologist who lived in Italy in the eighteen hundreds. He came up with a theory called anthropological criminology. Basically, he believed that criminality was an inherited trait and that he could tell who would become a criminal based on certain physical traits. Some of his theories were really wild. They've pretty much all been debunked now."

She grinned at him.

"What?"

"Sometimes I forget what a big nerd you are," she teased.

"Really? I never forget what a petite nerd *you* are, counselor," he teased her back.

She giggled, then grew more serious. "So, what's the tragedy in this guy's past that made him create a creepy computerized version of a crank criminologist?"

His smile faded. "His son was killed. It happened while he was still in California. The kid was in high school. He caught a bullet during a drug buy gone wrong. It's not clear whether he just happened to be in the wrong place or what. Either way, he bled out in an alley."

"Oh. That's horrible. And the shooter?"

"He was a two-time loser named Calvin Tennyson. The cops actually stopped him the night of the murder, but he played it cool. He skipped town, ended up getting stabbed to death in a domestic dispute of some kind in North Carolina a year or so later. But Lewis was obsessed. He's convinced that the death of his son could have been predicted and, thus, prevented."

She fell quiet and didn't speak until they were standing on the sidewalk in front of their house. As they mounted the steps, she said, "I can see how losing a child like that could mess a person up. I mean, my parents had a couple bad years after Patrick. And, even now ..."

"Even now?" he prompted as she trailed off.

"Well, unlike Mr. Lewis, who seems obsessed with knowing what happened, my parents seem committed to closing their eyes to the truth."

He reached out his hand and stopped her as she was turning her key in the door. "What does that mean?"

"I think my brother might have had an illegitimate child. I think Allie might have been pregnant with his baby when he died."

He gaped at her. He had too many questions competing for primacy. He didn't know where to start.

"Here, I took a picture this morning after I took Jordana home. Let me show you." As she pushed open the door and crossed the threshold into the living room, she pawed through her bag for her phone. "Hold this, please." She handed him the puppy dog snack pack and pulled out her phone.

He closed the door behind them and waited to see the picture she wanted to show him, but she was staring down at her text messages.

"Everything okay?"

"Yeah. I guess I got some texts while we were walking home. Charlie Robinson's been released, along with another man named Sam Blank. Raquel—Charlie's partner—says they're okay, but shaken. I need to call her real quick and set up a time to talk to them in the morning."

He recognized the look in her eyes. Her mind was spinning at top speed, churning out questions to ask, cases to consult, causes of action to bring. She was gearing up to throw herself into her case. And that was fine. But first she needed to unburden herself about Patrick.

"I'll walk the dog and feed the cat while you do that, but I want to hear about your brother as soon as you're off the phone. Okay?"

She nodded. "I'll tell you all about it before bed. I promise."

23

Sasha ended the call with Raquel and Charlie, went over her notes, and then sketched out a short agenda for their meeting tomorrow. Most of what Charlie had recounted squared with Connelly's explanation of Landon Lewis and his predictive policing program. She emailed Jordana some research questions to get started on when she had her feet back under her. Then she cracked her back, changed into pajamas, and did a short yoga wind-down sequence.

After she washed her face and brushed her teeth, she padded through her unusually quiet house in search of her husband and the pets. She found all three sound asleep on the couch in the living room. Connelly was sleeping hard, his arm flung over his eyes, his feet propped up on the ottoman, the cat curled into a comma on his lap. The dog nestled into his side, snoring softly.

He'd been awake as long as she had. She checked the time—almost midnight. It had been a twenty-plus-hour day. She yawned. No wonder he was crashed out.

She covered him with a warm blanket and turned out the lights. He would have carried her up to bed if the situation was reversed. But she had her limits. And carrying a six-foot-tall, hundred-and-seventy-five-pound man up a flight of stairs exceeded those limits. She brushed her lips over his forehead and tiptoed out of the room.

She crawled into bed, expecting to fall asleep the moment her head hit the pillow. Unfortunately, instead, her eyes popped open, and she stared, wide awake, at the ceiling. Part of her brain was working through the call with Charlie Robinson and the massive civil rights case they planned to file. Her inability to shut off her thoughts was a frequent side effect of working late at night.

But most of her mind was preoccupied with a

different topic entirely: Allie and Patrick. She combed through her memories, taking them out one by one and turning them over to examine them to see if they revealed hints or raised questions.

And, in retrospect, it was clear. Obvious. Hard to miss, even. Her brother and her roommate had been having an affair. And Allie had gotten pregnant.

That time she found Patrick hanging out in her childhood bedroom with Allie when she got home from her summer job early.

Or when Allie randomly scored a pair of tickets to game three of the American League Championship in Boston, just six weeks before Patrick died. As far as Sasha knew, Allie wasn't a baseball fan, but Patrick was. And he'd jumped at the chance to see Roger Clemens pitch. And Sasha had thought nothing of Allie and Patrick going to Boston together—because he always said Allie was like a second little sister.

And what about how sick and tired Allie was that entire Fall semester, sleeping in, skipping breakfast. Puking on the side of the road after the funeral. She hadn't been overcome by emotion. She'd been experiencing morning sickness.

So much suddenly made sense. Allie's heartbreak over Patrick's death, which had seemed a bit disproportionate at the time. Karyn's eruption when Sasha's mom read the Christmas card from Allie. And the way Allie dropped off the planet after Christmas. She never came back to campus, not even to clean out her room. Her parents had hired one of the maintenance men to box up her stuff and drive it to California in her little BMW. She never returned a single phone call, didn't answer any letters, acknowledge Sasha's emails. She cut off all communication.

At the time, Sasha assumed Allie wouldn't talk to her because she was embarrassed about dropping out. But maybe she'd been afraid she'd let it slip that she was pregnant and Patrick was the father.

Which meant, of course, that Sasha was the baby's aunt. He was her eldest nephew. And she had never met him. Her throat tightened, and she forced herself to take a centering breath.

She reached over and clicked on her bedside lamp. The only questions left were whether Allie had kept the baby or put him up for adoption and whether he knew who his father was.

She'd spent her day tracking down the wrong woman. She needed to find Allie, not Karyn, if she wanted answers. She made a note to do some basic social media profile searches in the morning to see if Allie was active anywhere. And, if not, she'd call the Georgetown alumni office after she met with Charlie and Sam Blank.

Having memorialized her next steps, she flicked off the light and nestled back into bed, hopeful that her mind would shut down and let her sleep now that she'd worked through it. She started counting backward from one hundred and only made it to sixty-seven before drifting off.

She stirred just once, when Connelly wandered into the room half-asleep and collapsed onto the bed next to her.

"Good night," he whispered.

"Mmm."

"I'm sorry I fell asleep before we could talk."

"In the morning," she mumbled into her pillow.

He kissed her neck and curled up beside her, one hand resting on her hip. "Love you."

"Love you more." She fell back to sleep to the sound of his even breathing.

24

Charlie woke up and stretched extravagantly. He was sore and stiff from the time spent in the cell, but the luxury of sleeping in his own bed had soothed most of his minor aches. A mattress, a pillow, a soft clean blanket, and the warm curves of the woman in his bed had washed away the rest of them.

He glanced over at Raquel and smiled. She was curled on her side, sleeping soundly, her hand resting on his hip. He eased her hand off and slipped out of the bed, taking care not to wake her. She'd spent a grim, sleepless night worrying about him; he owed it to her to let her sleep in. In fact, he decided, he'd make her breakfast before he met with the lawyer. School could wait. His students were adults; they'd understand if Rush taught today's seminar.

He crept toward the living room. Sam may not have his hearing, but in Charlie's experience, that would tend to mean he'd sleep very lightly rather than heavily. His Auntie Rae used to start awake the instant someone entered her room.

As he padded past the futon on his way to the kitchen to start the coffee, he frowned. The futon bed was still unfolded, but the sheets had been neatly stacked in a pile on the bottom, along with the fleece blanket Raquel had unearthed from the back of the closet. Sam, however, was nowhere to be seen.

He glanced down the hall and noted that the bathroom door was ajar. Sam wasn't in there.

He flipped on the kitchen light and spotted the note sitting beside the coffee maker. He picked it up and scanned it:

Charlie,

    Thank you for your hospitality. But we both know this isn't over yet with the Milltown PD. They won't stop until they have what they want.

*And I don't know what they want. I couldn't live
with myself if I brought any more trouble to you
and your woman. I'll be fine.*

    Power to the People,

    Sam

CHARLIE SWORE under his breath and returned
the note to its spot on the counter. Sam was right,
he knew. Whatever the Milltown Police Department wanted with Sam, it was unlikely to end
just because the hopped-up guy with the goon
squad had cut him loose.

All the same, the thought of Sam on the run
from the cops, with no fixed address and no one
to interpret for him, made Charlie feel queasy.
He abandoned his coffee and headed into the
bathroom.

Power to the People? Sam must be older than
he looked. That slogan went out in the late
sixties, early seventies at the latest.

He turned on the water in the shower full-
blast. While he waited for it to heat up, he
studied his reflection in the mirror. He looked
haggard, and, more than that, he looked like a

man who wanted to pretend everything was fine, just coast along under the radar and avoid trouble.

"No," he said aloud, biting off the word.

Some trouble was necessary. Good, even. And finding Sam and helping him was the kind of trouble worth getting into.

"No," he repeated.

Maybe the lawyer—his lawyer—would know how to track down Sam. Whether she did or not, he promised himself as he stepped into the steamy shower stall, he would find Sam Blank. No matter what.

He stepped into the shower stall and positioned himself under the spray. Hot, forceful water pounded down on him. He closed his eyes and washed away all thoughts of the cell, the guards, and, yes, even Sam. It was cleansing, cathartic, even. But as soon as he twisted the faucet to stop the flow of water, he felt guilty. Dirty again. Like a traitor. Because he'd so willingly cast Sam aside—even if only in his thoughts.

A Bible verse bubbled up, unbidden, into his consciousness:

> *Do not forsake your friend or the*
> *friend of your parent;*
> *do not go to the house of your kindred*
> *in the day of your calamity.*
> *Better is a neighbor who is nearby*
> *than kindred who are far away.*

It was from *Proverbs, 27:10*, if his memory served, and he knew it did. He'd spent too many Sunday mornings serving as an acolyte to misremember his Bible. The point of the verse—or at least the reason why it had come to mind—was the instruction not to rely on your brother, but to count on your friends. And to be a friend who can be counted on. Sam was a neighbor nearby, a man who shared an outlook with Charlie. *Power to the People.*

"I'm not going to leave you in the wind," he said aloud, even though he had no idea where Sam might be. But he made the promise as sincerely and full-throatedly as he'd done anything in his life.

25

Landon slept poorly. He detested being used, and he was fairly certain that's what was happening here. All night, his dreams had been filled with replays of the scene in the box. Robinson signing. Blank signing. Cesare. He was missing something. Something critical.

He woke before sunrise. Tired, not rested, but unable to sleep any longer. He stood and prowled around the room.

Why had Officer Willard insisted on including Sam Blank in the roundup? It made no sense. He wasn't dangerous—it was beyond dispute, and it was something Craig Willard would've known. He was a veteran officer. Until now, Landon would've said his judgment was impeccable.

Some people might have shrugged it off as an error, but not Landon. Whenever a piece of data didn't fit a pattern as expected, he didn't disregard it. He analyzed it, picking it apart until he either made it fit or understood why it didn't.

In this case, his best tool was the source of the outlying data. He'd simply ask Willard. He should wait until mid-morning, when Kara Diamond would be sure to be gone.

She'd made it plain that she—and, by extension, Chief Carlson—was unhappy that he hadn't kept Blank in detention. He sensed that she and the chief would be equally displeased to learn that he was poking at the decision to pick him up in the first place. He wasn't naïve: Willard would eventually report back to his superiors about his interactions with Landon. But there was no reason not to give himself a head start.

He drove to the gym, ran five miles on the track in dizzying circles, lifted weights. Then he showered, dressed, guzzled a bottle of water, and checked the time. Twenty past eight. Late enough, he decided.

He went out to the car and settled himself

behind the wheel. Before he pulled out, he connected his phone to his car's Bluetooth.

Then he punched in the Milltown Police Department's main number, started the engine, and waited. The line rang three times, then Paul Holtzman's distinctive voice crackled in his ear.

"Milltown PD."

"Officer Holtzman?"

"Yes. Who's this?" he countered warily.

"Landon, Landon Lewis."

"Oh, Mr. Lewis, hi. You looking for Chief Carlson? I can put you through."

"No, actually, I was hoping to chat with Officer Willard."

"Craig, uh, Officer Willard's out in the field, sir."

Of course. He'd been so eager to catch Willard when Diamond wasn't around that he hadn't considered he might not be at the station.

"Shoot. Could you radio him and have him call me?"

"Um ... well, I could, but it'll be a while before he'll be able to get back to you. He's actually doing crowd control today."

"Oh? Another protest?"

"Yes and no. There's an open carry group

picketing the mayor's office this morning. But we don't anticipate any problems from those guys, so we don't really treat it the same with the riot squad or anything. More like directing traffic, that sort of thing."

"I see."

"Any chance I could help you?"

He bit the inside of his check and weighed his options. Why not?

"Maybe. Did Officer Willard ever bring Sam Blank in—before Wedneday night, I mean? Are there any reports, anything that would explain why he identified Blank as a threat and bounced him to the PPC?"

There was a long, long pause.

Thinking that Paul either hadn't heard or hadn't understood the request, Landon opened his mouth to rephrase it. Just then, Paul said, "You mean Comford, right?"

"Pardon?"

"It wasn't Willard who tagged Sam Blank. It was Brittany Comford."

An image of the brunette officer at the front desk crystallized. Her name badge flashed in his mind's eye. "Comford? Was she the duty officer that night?"

"That's right."

"And you're positive? She's the one who fingered Blank?"

"Yeah, sure. I was there when they accessed the traffic camera. I heard her. She said he was a bad dude." The faint clacking of keys sounded through the line. Paul was looking something up on his computer. "But ... um ... I don't see any old reports in the system that indicate she had any previous encounters with him. How could she, really? She hasn't even been here a month."

"Oh?"

Paul lowered his voice conspiratorially. "Helluva thing, her being in an officer-involved shooting her first shift. She's been riding a desk ever since."

"What?"

"You know, that kid. The one they had the protest for."

"Are you saying ... She shot Vaughn Tabor?"

"Mmm-hmm."

"Huh."

"Is there anything else I can help you with?"

"No, you've been very helpful, Officer Holtz-man. Thank you."

He ended the call and scratched his neck, pondering his next move. Very helpful, indeed.

He merged onto the Liberty Bridge and pointed himself toward his office. He made a mental note to avoid the massive sinkhole that had swallowed a city bus just weeks earlier as he inched through the snarled traffic.

26

S asha arrived at Charlie Robinson's apartment ten minutes early for their meeting. She stayed in the car and checked emails, then scrolled through her social media apps. She'd found Allie—or at least she thought it was Allie—on two different sites and had sent a friend request to her profile on each.

Alexandra MacManus was the right age to be Allie and had attended, but not graduated from, Georgetown. Born in California. And she looked like an age-advanced version of the teenager Sasha had shared a dorm room with twenty years ago. Alexandra MacManus, if she was Allie, had her privacy settings fairly locked down. Sasha was unable to see who her friends and family members were, which made it a little harder to be sure she was right about the woman's identity.

She took pains to craft her messages to be vague enough that they wouldn't set off any alarms bells if this poor woman wasn't her old roommate and lighthearted enough that if it was Allie, she would have no reason not to respond. At least that's what Sasha hoped. So far, though, there hadn't been a response to either message, even though they both showed as having been read.

She shrugged. She'd done what she could do for now. It was time to compartmentalize her search for Patrick's (possible) son until after her meeting with Charlie Robinson and Sam Blank.

She glanced at the time, killed the engine, and removed her keys. As she was exiting the car, her cell phone vibrated. She pulled out the device and checked the display. It was a text from Connelly.

`Any word from Allie?`

```
                          Not yet.
                   But if she's in Cali,
               it's still pretty early.
```

```
True.
```

Her husband had been surprisingly accepting of her theory when she'd filled him in over breakfast. She'd expected him to tell her she was jumping to conclusions or straining the evidence to fit what she believed. Instead, he'd agreed that the student in the picture looked an awful lot like her brother. He'd also conceded that the timing lined up. If Patrick and Allie had, in fact, had an affair, the boy could be their son. And he seemed to think the circumstantial evidence pointed to a liaison. In short, he backed her theory. A theory that wasn't exactly air-tight. It was more like the colander of theories, punched full of loads of small holes.

Still, he was supporting her, and she'd take it. She wondered if the unexpected way his father had materialized in his life had anything to do with his reaction. He'd spent his teens and the better part of his twenties looking for his dad. One day, long after he'd given up the search in any meaningful way, a messenger appeared on their doorstep with a message. Duc Nguyen was dying of liver cancer and needed a transplant from his son to stay alive. The touching family reunion *did* lose some of its shine when Connelly learned that his father was a murderous gangster.

She could only hope that any introduction to Patrick and Allie's son—if that's who the kid was —would end on a happier note than had Connelly's meeting with his dad.

Another text pinged. She glanced down at it and smiled. Connelly had snapped a picture of Finn and Fiona, both tousle-haired and sleepy-eyed and still in their pajamas:

```
Leaving R & R's now.
Kids send their love.
See you soon.

                    Love you all.
```

She stowed the phone in her bag, wound her scarf around her neck to stave off the chill, and hurried up the stairs to Charlie Robinson's apartment building as a gust of cold wind caught the ends of the scarf and lifted them. One week out, the weather forecast was calling for snow for Thanksgiving.

Thanksgiving. *How would Mom do this year? Twenty years. This was a big one.*

She hadn't really interacted with her mom at the bonfire. She'd been convinced Valentina would have taken one look at her face and known she'd gotten into it with Riley and Jordan. The last thing she wanted to do was talk with her mother about Patrick's possible infidelity. At some point, she'd have to address it.

Now, though, she had a more pressing task. She pressed the buzzer for the Robinson/Jones apartment.

A voice crackled over the intercom. "Sasha?"

"Yes, it's me."

"Come on up."

A metallic buzz signaled the door unlocking. She stepped inside, welcoming the blast of over-heated air that hit her in the face. The elevator waited in the lobby, doors open. She walked past it to the stairway, pushed on the metal fire door, and took the stairs to the third floor two at a time.

She had just rapped her fist against the apartment door when her phone rang. The door opened as she pulled out her phone to answer the call. She didn't recognize the number.

"Sasha McCandless-Connelly," she said briskly.

At the same time, she held up one finger to indicate to the wiry man inside the door that she needed a minute. He nodded and ducked back inside, leaving the door open a crack for her.

"It's Allie Peterman. I understand you've been trying to get in touch with me."

She noted that Allie used her maiden name rather than confirm that she was, in fact, now known as Alexandra MacManus. Distancing language. But why?

"Allie, yes. I sent you some messages." She recalled their old friendship and smiled in an attempt to infuse her voice with warmth.

"What do you want?" Allie's voice was flat and icy.

So much for warmth. She'd give plainspoken truth a shot.

"Yesterday was the twentieth anniversary of Patrick's death. Obviously, that was on my mind, and, of course, that meant I was thinking about you, too."

When Allie answered, her voice had thawed, but only by a degree or two. "Wow, I guess it has been twenty years. But I'm not sure why you'd reach out to me now after all this time."

"I did try to get in touch with you after you left school. Didn't your parents give you any of my messages?"

"I don't remember. It's been a long time."

"Yeah, it has. But I've thought of you a lot over the years. I always wondered what happened to you and how you were doing. So you're married? Do you have any kids?"

"I'm going to say this plainly, Sasha. I don't wish you ill. But I'm not interested in resuming our friendship. I called simply to let you know that so you wouldn't harbor any fantasy about us reconnecting."

Well. There was no reason not to go for it now. "Is that because you were sleeping with my brother when he died?"

That was a long silence, then Allie said stiffly, "I beg your pardon?"

"I'm pretty sure you heard me."

"I'm not going to dignify that with a response."

Sasha plowed ahead, hurrying to get her

questions out before Allie hung up on her. "Were you pregnant, Allie? At Patrick's funeral, did you know you were carrying his baby? Or did you find out later, maybe when you went home for Christmas break? Is that why you didn't come back to school?"

"Listen carefully. If you ever contact me again, I will sue you into oblivion. Leave me alone, and leave my family alone." Allie's voice shook with fury as she ended the call.

Sasha took a moment to let the rush of cortisol wash through her. The call had been tense and combative, but it had served its purpose. Allie's reaction—and the crucial fact that she hadn't outright denied any of Sasha's accusations—confirmed that she was on the right track. Allie had been sleeping with Patrick. And she'd gotten pregnant.

Sasha thought making progress would bring a feeling of vindication. Instead, she felt lousy. Unsettled and rattled.

Put it away for now. It's time to focus on Charlie's issue.

Sasha pushed open the door to Charlie Robinson and Raquel Jones' apartment and stepped inside. It was warm and homey and smelled like cinnamon spice. Charlie and Raquel sat at a small oak table, each cradling a cup of coffee in their hands. Charlie stood.

"Can I get you a coffee or a glass of water?" he asked.

"I'd love a coffee, black. Can I just hang this here?" She unbuttoned her coat and gestured to the rack inside the door.

"Please," Raquel said.

She unwound her scarf and hung her coat and scarf from the hook, then joined them in the kitchen. Charlie handed her a glazed ceramic mug of steaming hot coffee.

"Thank you." She wrapped her hands around it to warm them.

"Is everything okay?" Charlie asked. "Your call sounded liked it got kinda heated."

"We weren't listening on purpose, promise. But the acoustics here are weird. Your voice carried," Raquel broke in.

Sasha pasted on a smile. "No worries. That call was about an unrelated matter. I'm sorry you had to hear that. I'll put my phone away in a moment while we talk. But before we get started, professor, can I just ask you a question? It relates to that other matter."

He wrinkled his brow and threw her a puzzled look. "Sure?" he said, his voice rising at the end.

"Thanks." She handed him the picture she'd snapped of Patrick's double in front of the library. "This is a long shot, but do you happen to know this student? Maybe you've had him in one of your classes?"

He studied the picture, then shook his head slowly. "No. He's not one of my students. Looks familiar, though. But I can't place him, sorry." He handed the phone back to her.

"Thanks for looking." She stowed the phone, disappointed but not surprised.

"Hang on. Was that photograph taken in front of the library?"

"It was." Her traitorous heart ticked up a beat.

He nodded. "Yeah, I don't know his name. But he works in the library. That's where I know him from. I'm sure of it. I've seen shelving books and once or twice at the circulation desk. If you need to interview him or whatever, you could probably find him there."

Her pulse went wild. She called on her meditation training and her Krav Maga-practiced calm to wrestle it back into line. "Thanks. That's very helpful." She scanned the cozy room. "Is Mr. Blank not joining us?"

Charlie and Raquel exchanged a long glance. Raquel walked to the kitchen, picked up a sheet of paper that was sitting on the counter beside the coffee maker, and handed it to Sasha.

As she skimmed the short note, Charlie said, "He was gone when I woke up this morning. He left that."

"What does he mean about the Milltown PD not being finished with him?"

Another look passed between the couple.

She leaned forward, "As we discussed last night on the phone, I'm your attorney. I'm representing you. Anything you share with me is confidential. You can tell me."

"Sam was there," Charlie said simply.

"I don't understand."

"He was on the scene when Vaughn Tabor was killed. He ran, but the cops, they saw him."

She was quiet for a long moment. "Last night,

we discussed a cause of action centered on improper profiling. This is ... something different."

"I know. And they did that. That happened. But also, this is—I ... we have to help Sam." Charlie stopped and grimaced in frustration.

Raquel placed her hand on his arm and rubbed it. She spoke in a soothing tone. "Listen, Charlie. Just slow down, babe. Start at the beginning and tell Ms. McCandless-Connelly everything that happened with Sam." She cut her eyes toward Sasha. "Right?"

"Exactly right," she encouraged. "And don't leave anything out. Don't edit or censor yourself, Charlie. Don't make any judgments about what's important to the case or most helpful to Sam. Okay? I need you to just tell me your story."

He let out a shaky breath. "Okay. Yeah, I can do that."

She gave him an encouraging smile. "Great. Now, I'm going to take some notes. I don't want to distract you so just keep talking." She removed a legal pad and a pen from her bag and settled in at the table.

Most of what Charlie went over tracked what

he said on the phone the previous night, and they moved quickly through the retelling.

All the men who'd been taken into the van were minorities. The students were all let go. But he, Mr. Barefoot, and Mr. Blank were detained, and, eventually, each of the three was interviewed by the man in charge.

"The man who was in charge, did you catch a name?"

"No," Charlie answered.

She took a folder from her bag and slid it across the table. "Is this him?"

Charlie opened the folder and gaped down at the photograph she'd printed from Landon Lewis' now-defunct NetworkUp profile page. He looked at her as if she were a magician.

"Yes! He's a bit older, but this is definitely the guy."

"His name is Landon Lewis."

"Do you recall any details of his predictive policing program that you didn't mention when we spoke yesterday?

He went quiet, thinking, then shook his head. "No. I told you everything last night. Oh, except he mentioned somebody named Cesare."

She shook her head. "Cesare isn't a person,

it's a program—or an artificial intelligence, more accurately."

"Cesare is the AI that tagged me as someone with latent criminality?"

"Yes. He calls it a predictive and preventive crime tool."

"PPC," Raquel interjected. "That's probably what it stands for, predictive and preventive crime."

Sasha laughed softly. "It probably is. Thanks for pointing that out; it's been bothering me. So, Mr. Lewis told you that the AI identified you, Mr. Blank, and Mr. Barefoot all as individuals who were predicted to commit serious crimes?"

"Something like that. Barefoot's an ex-con. My arrests have mainly related to my protest activities."

She noted the use of the qualifier *'mainly'* but let it pass without comment.

"And Mr. Blank?"

"Sam relieved himself on a tree."

"Pardon?"

"He had an outstanding warrant for public urination. Which, you know, is total BS."

"So he believed the real reason he was picked

up was because he witnessed Vaughn Tabor's shooting?"

Charlie pursed his lips and eyed her. "You don't?"

"I don't care to jump to conclusions. But I also don't believe in coincidences. So let's just say it smells bad."

"You mean it reeks," Raquel corrected her.

"Who else knew?"

"I told Barefoot, but nobody else was around. By that point, the students had been released. The guards—Fox and Scott—were stationed outside the hallway where our cell was. So they couldn't have heard. I mean ... at least not in real time."

"What do you mean by that? Do you think you may have been recorded?

He shrugged. "Maybe. There was a ceiling-mounted camera, but we all kept our backs to it most of the time. And I don't know if there's an audio feed. But we kept things pretty quiet. I think we can assume nobody else knows."

"Except for the cops who shot Vaughn, you mean." Raquel's voice was a knife's edge.

"She has a point. Surely they told Lewis why they wanted Sam to be detained."

Charlie traced circles on the table with his finger. "I don't think they did. That Lewis guy seemed baffled. His Cesare program didn't flag Sam as a 'latent criminal.' And peeing in a park? I mean, come on. But he didn't ask anything about the shooting. He kept trying to get at what the real reason was because public urination didn't hold water."

"Neither did Sam."

Raquel's crack lightened the mood, and Charlie's face brightened for a moment. When he finished laughing, his eyes grew serious. "As horrific as that detention center was, I think Sam might have been safer there than he is on the streets. Lewis and his goons are nightmare fuel, but at least they have some, I don't know, internal code they follow. Milltown PD, though ..."

He trailed off, but he didn't need to finish the sentence. They were all thinking the same thing.

Sasha drained her coffee mug, then said, "Okay, but surely Sam knew that he wouldn't be safe if he left your place. So why did he bolt? You think someone got to him?"

"Nah, he was crashed out on the futon when I went to bed. I think he just woke up spooked. I mean, he knows why he got picked up, and he's right: if the police department wants to silence him, they aren't gonna stop just because this PPC program cut him loose."

"And he didn't tell you what he saw—that night, I mean?"

Charlie shook his head. "Nah."

She doodled a snowflake in the corner of her notepad. "Okay, last night, I proposed filing a civil rights complaint against Lewis and the PPC. That's a long shot because of all the secrecy around the program. Realistically, the best chance of success would be to name the Milltown Police Department as a codefendant under the theory that they must be collaborating with Lewis. Last night, I thought that was awfully tenuous. But then I saw Landon Lewis' picture."

"And?" Charlie asked, wrinkling his brow.

"And I realized I'd seen him before. When I went to get Jordana from the police station, he was coming in when we were leaving. He held the door for us. At the time, I assumed one of the other protestors had also called a lawyer. But it was him. So I think we have a basis to name the PD."

She left unsaid the wrinkle that if she ended up being a fact witness, she wouldn't be able to represent Charlie and the others. With any luck, Jordana would remember seeing him, too. She could testify if needed.

One thing at a time.

"How does that help Sam?"

"It doesn't help him in the short term. Right now, we need to find him. But once we sue the police department, they'll be under a spotlight, more than they already are, I mean. That alone should provide some protection for Sam. Nobody takes out a witness when everyone is watching."

The Milltown district attorney was investigating the shooting of Vaughn Tabor, but the investigation was moving slowly and out of the eye of the public. If she sued the department in federal court for civil rights violations, she could make a lot of noise.

Charlie shuddered at the notion of the police silencing Sam permanently. She hated to be so blunt, but that was the end game, and they all knew it.

"Okay, so what's our next step? Finding Sam?"

"Finding Sam is key. But I also want to get a placeholder complaint on file with the district court today. That puts the police department and the PPC on notice that their behavior is being scrutinized."

"Couldn't it also push them to take action against Sam even faster?"

"It could," she allowed. "Our next step is a gamble, either way. But we can't do nothing."

Charlie glanced at Raquel. She nodded.

He inhaled and pushed back his shoulders. "Okay. Let's do it."

"Come on, then. Let's go talk to Max Barefoot and see if he'll join the complaint." She stood and pushed in her chair.

"Now?"

"No time like the present."

"I hope we're making the right choice," Charlie mused as he handed her her coat from the rack.

So did she.

27

Sasha came to a stop and pointed across the street to a small red brick home on the outskirts of Milltown, not far from the bypass leading into Pittsburgh.

"This is it."

Charlie peered at the house with its lace living room curtains and the neat row of box hedges lining the front porch. "It's hard to imagine Barefoot living in a place like this."

"According to the property records, it was his grandmother's place. She died when he was in prison, and he inherited it," Sasha told him. "You ready?"

He nodded. She popped the locks, and they exited the vehicle. They hurried across the street, collars upturned against the blast of cold air, and raced up to the porch. She jabbed the doorbell while Charlie jammed his bare hand into his pockets and stamped his feet to keep the blood flowing.

After a few moments, footsteps sounded in the hallway, and a shadow appeared behind the frosted glass door. The person on the other side of the door shifted to get a good look at them through a clear pane in the sidelight glass.

"Come on, man, it's cold out here," Charlie protested.

Sasha turned and casually glanced across the street. She hoped Barefoot would hurry up, too. But not because of the cold.

"Hang on," came the muffled response from inside, followed by the sound of a lock scraping across its barrel. And then the door swung open.

"Hey, man," Charlie said.

"What are you doing here?" Barefoot countered.

Sasha stepped forward. "Mr. Barefoot, hi. I'm Sasha McCandless-Connelly. I'm an attorney representing Professor Robinson and Mr. Blank. Could we please come inside? Please?" She allowed a note of urgency to creep into her voice.

She could feel Charlie giving her a sidelong look, but she ignored it. They needed to get inside. Now.

Barefoot shuffled back to give them room to cross the threshold. "Yeah, okay, I guess, come on in. You want a drink or anything?" His tone made it clear that the only acceptable answer was no.

He shut the door behind them. She was pleased to see that he re-engaged the lock.

"No, thank you. I was hoping to talk to you a bit about your experience at the PPC detention center."

"The what?"

"The place where you were held is called the PPC. It probably stands for Predictive and Preventive Crime or something similar."

He barked out a laugh. "That dude, the one who looked like a banker or something, he kept going on about some technology that knew I was gonna commit more crimes."

"Right. His name is Landon Lewis, and he's invented an artificial intelligence program that he says can predict latent criminality based on some proprietary blend of factors."

Barefoot twisted his mouth. "A blend of factors like having black skin and being a man."

Sasha allowed herself a faint smile. "That goes to the heart of the matter. Professor Robinson and Mr. Blank plan to file a lawsuit in federal court suing the PPC and the Milltown Police Department for violations of their civil rights. You would also have those same causes of action if you'd like to join them. But there's a wrinkle."

"Oh, let me guess. You want paid up front."

Charlie jumped in, "No, it's nothing like that. Her firm is doing this pro bono, which means—"

"I know what it means. I've had free legal representation a time or two. Criminal law clinic up at the law school. So what's the wrinkle, then?"

"The wrinkle is that Mr. Blank went missing last night," Sasha told him.

Barefoot's eyes widened. "Come on in and sit down." He ushered them into a living room decorated by his late grandmother—either that, or he had a fondness for lace doilies and clear plastic couch protectors.

Sasha settled herself on the loveseat amidst a loud crackle of plastic. Charlie sat next to her, and Max Barefoot claimed the corduroy recliner.

"Sam's missing?"

Charlie cleared his throat. "He came back to my place after they sprang us. I told him he could stay as long as he wanted, but he must've freaked in the middle of the night. He was gone when I woke up."

"That's not missing. That's he rolled," Barefoot corrected him.

Charlie scoffed. "Come on, man. You know what he saw. The police are gonna come looking for him, and it's gonna be bad if they find him before we do."

Their host cut his eyes towards Sasha, then looked back at Charlie. "I don't know what he saw. I don't know anything about that." His eyes were marbles, hard and cold.

"Mr. Barefoot, as I'm sure you're well aware, if you engage me as your attorney in the civil rights matter, anything you say to me about your time at the PPC will be covered by attorney-client privilege." Sasha tried not to let her impatience bleed through, but they didn't have time for this feigned ignorance routine.

"I'm not sure I want to get involved."

Charlie made a snarling sound, and Sasha shot him a warning look.

"That's understandable. But, you should

know that even if you don't join the lawsuit, they're not going to leave you alone."

"What are you talking about?"

She unstuck her bottom from the plastic and stood up. "Did you notice that your house is under surveillance?"

"What?" He jumped to his feet.

She led him to the window and shifted the lace curtain. Charlie squeezed in beside them.

"Look across the street. Do you see that navy blue Suburban behind the gray station wagon?" she asked.

"Yeah, I see it."

"It's been there since we got here. There are two men with buzz cuts, dressed head to toe in black just sitting in the front seat, drinking coffee, looking at your house."

"You think they're plainclothes?" Barefoot asked as he twitched the curtain back into place. They all moved away from the window.

"No. There's no way Milltown could afford a fleet of Suburbans. Those are Lewis' men."

"Damn," Charlie breathed.

"My suspicion is they're not going to let you out of their sight until they find something to prove their algorithm right."

"They're gonna stalk me?"

"They'll call it surveilling you, but yeah. They probably already have a wiretap on your phone, maybe on your computer."

"I didn't do anything."

"Their AI says you will."

"That's ... this is an invasion of privacy or something. This isn't right."

"No, it's not." She gave him a long look. "So, do you want to do something about it or not?"

He huffed out a breath. "Yeah, okay. Where do I sign?"

She reached into her bag and retrieved a blank engagement letter. "Read that. Let me know if you have any questions."

He skimmed it and held out his hand for a pen.

"Are you sure you don't want to read it more closely?"

"You're going to sue those rats sitting on my house, right?"

"Yes."

"And the cops who are working with them?"

"Yes."

"Let's make it happen. Give me a pen."

She handed him a ballpoint, and he rested the letter against the wall to scrawl his signature.

"Here."

"I'll have someone from my office send you a copy of this later today so you'll have it for your records." She slipped the sheet back into her bag and stuck out her hand to shake on it. He had a surprisingly gentle handshake.

"Hey," he said.

"Yes?"

"What should I do if they just, you know, bust in here without a warrant?"

"The pair in the car? I doubt they'd try it. They have to know they have no authority."

"No, I mean the cops."

"If the police show up with a search warrant, call me *immediately*." She searched his face to be sure he was hearing her.

"Okay. And if they show up without one, what do I do?"

"Don't let them in. They can't use evidence they obtain without a warrant anyway," she told him.

He laughed darkly. "Yeah, right. The Milltown Police do it all the time. They walk right in, search the joint, no warrant. Defense attorney tries to keep out the evidence, and the DA makes some fancy argument about, I don't know, it would be discovered no matter what? Next thing you know, the judge is letting it in."

She frowned. "They claim an inevitable discovery exception?"

"Yeah, that's what they called it. It happened in my trial. They searched my house, no warrant, and found the driver's license of the guy I jacked in my junk drawer."

Charlie scoffed. "Why'd you keep it?"

Barefoot shrugged. "Thought I could sell it, you know, to somebody who needed papers. Ended up landing my butt in a cell. The DA said the license would've led back to me inevitably when I sold it on the street."

Sasha shook her head. "That's not how the doctrine of inevitable discovery works. Or it's not how it's supposed to work, at least."

He shrugged. "I don't know what to tell you. I did a seven-year stretch, so it worked. But, okay. If they show up, I'll call you. What are you gonna do now?"

"Charlie and I are going to look for Sam. Any ideas where he hangs out?"

"No. But you should try the library. Those

guys always hang out there when it's cold outside."

"That's a good idea," Charlie said.

"What about those two?" Max jutted his chin toward the window.

Sasha smiled. "If you get bored, go outside and wander around. Lead them on a wild goose chase. They deserve it."

28

The mobile phone vibrated on Landon's desk. He grabbed it and looked at the display. Team Three, the men assigned to watch Barefoot.

"Do you have something?" he demanded by way of greeting.

Bartone, the senior agent on Team Three, waffled. "Maybe, sir."

"Maybe?"

"We're set up across the street from the target's residence. It's been quiet. He walked to the corner store earlier, came back with milk and a bag of groceries. A neighbor stopped by briefly. They spoke on the porch. We planted a transmitter on the underside of his mailbox, but we may need to reposition it—it failed to pick up the entire conversation clearly, but it seemed to involve a shared tree that's rotting. The neighbor is concerned the next big snowstorm will bring it down."

Landon pressed the fingers of his right hand against his forehead and pushed hard against the tension headache that was forming. "I hope you have more than that. Otherwise, just save it for the field report, Bartone."

Bartone hurriedly continued, "Yes, sir. There's more. After the neighbor departed and the target returned inside, a gray station wagon approached from the north and parked in front of us, directly opposite Mr. Barefoot's residence. There's only parking on one side of the street on Thursdays. Street cleaning."

"Feel free to edit out the unnecessary details." Landon could do without the play-by-play.

"Yes, sir. A petite female and a man we've confirmed is Charlie Robinson exited the vehicle. They approached the residence. Unfortunately, again, the broadcasting device didn't pick up most of the conversation on the porch. We'll get that taken care of the next time the subject leaves the home. In any event, he invited them inside. They're still in there. Should we call the Milltown PD?"

"Why would you do that, agent?"

"Sir, Robinson and Barefoot were not known associates before their time in the PPC. It's clear they formed some sort of alliance or relationship during their detention. That seems ... troubling, sir."

Landon drummed his fingers on the desk. "Yes, it's less than ideal that Robinson and Barefoot are meeting, but socializing isn't a crime in itself. I'm interested to know who this woman is. You said she drives a gray station wagon, and she's a small woman?"

"Affirmative and affirmative. She can't be but five feet tall."

The attorney who'd bailed out the blue-haired student was a tiny thing. And she drove a dark gray station wagon. His headache intensified.

"Run the plate."

"Forman's on it, sir. But, again, if we call in the address to the PD, Chief Carlson will authorize a search. He won't hesitate to send out officers."

"On what grounds? Having visitors isn't a justification for a search warrant. What's going on in Carlson's department?"

"Uh, sir, we've heard from some of the officers that they don't bother with search warrants much."

Landon encouraged his teams to get friendly with their law enforcement counterparts. Personal relationships made it easier to convince the local departments and units to accept the Cesare beta program and to trust the data. He hoped he wouldn't grow to regret his cozy relationship with the Milltown Police Department. There were plenty of small departments in the communities surrounding Pittsburgh that were completely clean and above board. He didn't want to think that he'd tethered himself, and his program, to a dirty one.

"Search warrants aren't optional, son. The United States Constitution protects citizens from unreasonable search and seizure."

Bartone laughed nervously. "I'm not a lawyer, sir."

"Neither am I. And yet, it behooves me to understand the letter of the law so that I can comply with it. It would behoove you to do the same."

"Uh, yes, sir. I'll bone up on the rules of evidence this weekend," Bartone promised. "But do you want me to call Milltown and have them break up this party or no?"

Irritation and worry mixed in a toxic brew, driving the band of pain behind his eyes to new heights. He gritted his teeth to keep from snapping. "Did the license plate come back yet?"

There was a mumbled back-and-forth between Bartone and his partner. After a moment, Bartone said, "the car is registered to a Sasha McCandless-Connelly."

"Ms. McCandless-Connelly is an attorney. So, you tell me? Do you think it's a good idea to call the Milltown PD and ask them to conduct an illegal search of a home where an attorney is present?"

"No, sir."

"Good answer. I'm pleased to learn that your brain hasn't fallen completely out of your head."

The agent wisely ignored the jab. "Assuming the lawyer and Robinson leave together and Barefoot stays home, do you want us to follow her or stay on him?"

Landon considered the question. He would like to know what she was up to. But he hadn't planned to surveil Robinson so closely. He couldn't let his curiosity distract him from his actual priorities.

"Stay with Barefoot. Put a tracker on her car."

"Yes, sir." Bartone passed along the order to Forman. Landon heard a car door slam, and, a moment later, it slammed again.

"Is it done?"

"It's done."

Technology was a beautiful thing. All Forman had to do was stick a relatively inexpensive, small magnetic GPS tracker to the underside of the lawyer's car. A ten-second job, and now Landon would know where she was at all times.

"Good. I'll have Marshall's team monitor her."

Bartone's voice came over the line again, crackling with urgency. "They've exited the residence, sir. Barefoot is still inside. Robinson returned to the station wagon. But she's approaching our vehicle, sir. Here she comes. She's tapping on the window. Now she's gesturing for me to roll it down. What should I do, sir?"

"Lower the window, agent. And get a grip on your emotions."

Could she have seen Forman? Surely the man had been discreet. He strained to listen to the back-and-forth between Bartone and the attorney. He could make out a female voice, but not the words. Bartone sounded like he was stammering.

After a seemingly interminable time, Bartone came back on the line. "Sir?" His voice was full of dread.

"Yes." Landon steeled himself to hear that she knew about the GPS tracker.

"She gave me her business card, sir. And she ... well, she said to tell you that she wants copies of her clients' nondisclosure agreements, sir. She's representing all three men."

He let out a whoosh of air. That wasn't too bad. The PPC had defended the program before, and it could do it again.

"You mean she said to tell me, as in, tell your superior?" he clarified.

"No, sir, she used your name. I don't know how she made us. I'm sorry."

The pain exploded behind Landon's eyes in a fireworks display of light and heat. He gripped the phone and squeezed his eyes shut. A blown surveillance detail was a minor concern at this point. How did this woman know who he was? And what else did she know?

29

Sasha settled into her seat behind the steering wheel and glanced over at Charlie. He looked clammy.

"Are you okay?"

"You just … went up to those guys? Why? You really think Lewis will call you?"

She shrugged. "Probably not. But now he knows I know who he is. If nothing else, he's gonna sweat for a while. Guys like Lewis count on hiding in the shadows, dwelling in secrecy. It'll throw him off-balance to feel exposed. It's not much of an advantage, but it's something."

"I guess," he said, unconvinced.

She knew from experience that Connelly and

Hank hated any shred of attention that came their way. Why would Lewis be any different?

But she couldn't very well explain that she knew what she was talking about because her husband worked for a secret government program that didn't officially exist. So she changed the subject instead.

"Have you heard anything about these warrantless searches that Max mentioned? You know, they did the same thing at your office while you were in detention."

He lifted his shoulders. "I don't know. Can't the prosecutors always get in what they need? I mean, judges bend over backward to help them all the time."

She wrinkled her nose as if she could smell the argument. "It happens, sure. The prosecution is often viewed as the good guys, but, Charlie, this is more than that. The right to be free from unreasonable searches and seizures is in the Constitution. It's a federally guaranteed constitutional right, for crying out loud."

"There are exceptions, though, right?"

"Some. They're limited, though. The whole reason the exclusionary rule provides that illegally obtained evidence can't be used at trial is to discourage the authorities from engaging in the abuses in the first place. To get improperly obtained evidence admitted under the inevitable discovery exception, the prosecution has to show that it would've been discovered in the same condition it was found in as the result of an independent investigation that was already underway when it was illegally seized. That's a high burden, Charlie. And a driver's license shoved in a kitchen drawer doesn't meet it."

He gave her a look that was almost pitying. "I don't want to say you sound naïve, but you're talking to a man who was grabbed off the street and held in a basement by some dudes who have no legal authority of any kind. Do you really believe the system always works?"

She nodded. It was a fair point. "Listen, if I drop you at the library to see if anyone knows where Sam might go, can you find a way home?"

"Yeah, no problem. Raquel can pick me up, or I'll catch a bus. Why, though? What are you going to do?"

She pulled out and headed for the library. She waved goodbye to the surveillance team in her rearview mirror. The guy on the driver's side of the Suburban flashed her the bird. Lovely.

"I need to check something out. If you get any leads on Sam's whereabouts, text me and also call my office. Ask to speak to Naya Andrews."

"Who's she? Your assistant?"

"No, she's a transactional partner, specializing in private equity offerings, but she's also the finest investigator I've ever met. If anyone can help us locate Sam, it's Naya."

"But you're not going back to the office?"

"Not right away."

He gave her a curious look but didn't press her any further.

The library was only a short trip from Max Barefoot's place on the edge of town. It was a tired-looking, blocky gray building. But libraries could be deceptive that way. Whether they were enormous white marble monuments to books guarded by verdigris copper lions or modest, underfunded community centers, they all shared one thing in common—there was an endless world inside. Of books, sure; but sometimes also computers, printers, tools, seeds, and toys. And, always, people who wanted to use their knowledge to help their neighbors. If anyone knew where Sam was, they were likely to be at the library.

She watched Charlie adjust his backpack onto his shoulders and lope up the library's wide front steps. Once he disappeared inside the building, she opened her mapping app to get directions to the spot where Vaughn Tabor had been killed.

She couldn't quite explain, even to herself, why she wanted to go there. Or why she didn't want to take Charlie with her. But she did, and she didn't, and she'd learned a long time ago to trust her instincts. Today, those instincts were telling her she needed to see the spot.

She thumbed out a quick text to Naya:

> Two things.
> 1. New client Charlie Robinson might call you. Trying to find a man named Sam Blank. No last known address. If CR has any leads, he'll reach out. You can use Jordana to do the legwork on

this, but I wd really
appreciate your help.
2. Have someone search for
all cases since 2009 where
Milltown DA has argued
inevitable discovery to get
around the exclusionary rule.
It's for the Robinson matter,
so bill it to the pro bono
client number.

Naya responded immediately:

Got it. You coming in?

Y. Later, though.
I have to take care of
something.

K. Bring some sugary coffee
thing with you. Or else.

Thanks for the warning.

She laughed and rested the phone in the
center console. She left the radio off and drove to

the intersection in silence, reviewing what she knew about the shooting. Not much, honestly. But she did know roughly where Vaughn Tabor had been standing. She could walk through the scene to get a sense of where Sam might have been.

She pulled over on the shoulder, nudging her car as close to the wooded county lot as she could. The road curved sharply, and she wasn't really interested in having her car sideswiped while she was poking around.

She left her bag sitting on the back seat and her cell phone charging in the console. Her shoes crunched loudly over the gravel, and a formation of migrating geese honked overhead. She kept her eyes down as she paced slowly across the space toward a makeshift memorial set up against a bright yellow sign with a thick black chevron.

She studied the teddy bears, cards, and candles piled in front of the sign's metal post, then let her eyes drift back to the ground. When she saw the faint chalk outline that indicated where Tabor had fallen, she crouched beside it and scanned the surrounding area. Where had Sam been?

She wished Aroostine were here. She would know. The prosecutor turned tracker could see things in the environment that Sasha never would.

She sighed. No, she might not know whether a squirrel had stopped to dig up a nut near the body, but she did have her own talents. Time to use them. She rocked back on her heels, closed her eyes, and tried to picture the action. If the police officers had been coming from Milltown, they would've approached from the same direction she just had. They fired, and Vaughn fell this way ... she opened her eyes and blinked. Sam had been in the woods. He had to have been.

She pivoted and stared into the neglected lot. It was scrabbly, with thick, overgrown, choking weeds and stunted, sparse trees and shrubs. And lots of trash. Cans, bottles, bags, and fast food wrappers, and abandoned protest signs were scattered through the weedy grass. She walked toward the lot and peered down into the underbrush, looking for ... something, she wasn't sure what exactly. But she'd know it when she saw it.

Then she heard tires squealing. She turned. A black van careened toward her. Reflexively, she threw herself into the weeds and out of the path of the van. It took several seconds to form the thought that a black van was bad news. Once her brain made the connection, it sent out a series of electrical impulses that instructed her legs to get moving. She scrambled to her feet and sprinted into the trees.

Deep voices shouted, ordering her to stop. She ran faster. The thud of heavy boots thrashing through the weeds and pounding against the hard earth sounded behind her. She ran faster still, her arms pumping, her hair shaking loose from the knot at the nape of her neck. Brambles tore at her face and neck, leaving long red scratches in their wake. She blinked away the blood and kept running.

Her scarf caught on a bare tree branch, pulling her backward. She yanked the scarf from her neck and ran on. As she raced through the woods, she risked a blurred backward glance at her pursuers. There were three of them. All dressed in black.

As she turned back, the stiletto heel of her left boot sank into the soft, muddy earth. Her ankle wobbled, wrenching her back, and she landed hard on the wet ground, her hands splayed out in front of her. The pounding of the boots grew louder. She yanked on her boot with both hands, but the heel was stuck. She fumbled with the zipper with shaking fingers, prepared to leave the boot in the mud and hobble on without it, but a tree-trunk-sized arm wrapped around her waist and its owner hoisted her up. Her boot came free.

She kicked and thrashed at the man, trying to reach his eyes with her fingernails. He just stretched out his arm and held her up at a distance. He chuckled, and her fear withered, replaced by an explosive eruption of impotent rage. He was a giant, an enormous slab of muscle, with a wingspan to match. She couldn't reach him.

He hefted her unceremoniously over his shoulder, like he was Santa Claus and she was a sack of Christmas presents. She allowed herself to go limp, her arms hanging listlessly over his back. She slowed her breathing and tried to focus the way her Krav Maga instructor would. And she waited for an opening. She willed herself to believe there would be an opening.

There's always an opening. You just have to be alert enough to spot it, Daniel's voice sounded in her mind.

When they reached the other two members of his team, she realized with horror that the giant carrying her was the runt of the litter. These guys were gargantuan.

The bigger they are, the harder they fall. The taunt she used to fling at her brothers when they tormented her sprang to mind, and she laughed despite her situation.

"If you think this is funny, what comes next is really gonna amuse you," the tallest of the three told her.

She stopped laughing and pressed her lips together.

When they emerged from the woods onto the berm of the road, she'd gathered her thoughts sufficiently to act. Her car was less than twenty feet away, unlocked. All she needed was one unguarded second. She lifted her head to her captor's ear, opened her mouth, and screamed, a loud, wild, hysterical scream.

"Holy shit!" He jumped and dropped her like she was on fire. She hit the ground, still screaming, and aimed a kick directly at his kneecap. Her angle sucked, and gravity wasn't on her side, but she put everything she had into it and drove her boot into the squishy cartilage of his patella.

He roared and pivoted away from her. She popped to her feet and started to run. The tall one grabbed the back of her coat and dragged her toward the van. She screamed again.

"Shut up." He pulled her closer and clamped his gloved hand over her mouth.

She bit down hard, but the thick leather protected the tender webbing between his thumb and pointer finger. He backhanded her across the cheek with his free hand.

"Bitch is feral," he fumed. A pair of handcuffs materialized from his belt. He cuffed her hands together and pushed her into the van. The men crowded in around her, one on each side, and the tall one in front. A fourth man was already behind the wheel, with the engine idling.

"She's feisty," he observed.

Sasha clamped her mouth shut and looked at her car. It was sitting *right* there. She'd been so close to getting away. And nobody knew where she was. Nobody would know where to look for her. A cold finger of fear slithered down into the pit of her stomach. She bounced her head back against the padded headrest and closed her eyes. Her cheekbone stung. Her ankle throbbed. She was surrounded by brutal giants.

And the worst thing of all—the absolute, most terrible part of her current predicament— was that if she managed to get out of this alive, Connelly would never let her live down the fact that it was her famously impractical taste in shoes that had landed her in this mess.

30

Sasha leaned toward her right and angled herself against the bars of the cell as best she could with her legs shackled and a chain running from her ankles to her waist, where her wrists were cuffed. She'd found that if she got her position exactly right, she'd be able to see the far outer door swing open even before she heard the pair of guards clomping down the hallway. She wasn't sure how that early warning was useful to her, given her physical contrasts, but she liked having it.

She assumed the guards were Fox and Scott, based on the descriptions that Charlie had given her. Whoever they were, they hadn't been in the van. They were two large men, but they were nothing compared to the super-sized bunch that had grabbed her. Which made sense. If she were an evil mastermind running an illegal detention operation, she'd send her biggest guys out to grab people off the street. Once you had someone chained up in a cell, you didn't really need much in the way of muscle to keep them in line.

She shifted her weight and decided it was the perfect time to meditate. Her Buddhist friend Bodhi had always told her that her biggest problem was she always had somewhere else to be. Currently, while there were many other places she wanted to be, there was nowhere else she could be. Might as well pass the time doing a lovingkindness meditation. She started with Finn and Fiona's sweet faces and called up the images of her family, one by one, and then her friends and coworkers and wished each of them well. Bodhi said you were supposed to end a lovingkindness meditation by first wishing people who annoyed you well, and then wishing your enemies well. She figured that was advanced meditation, and stopping while she was ahead was good enough for a beginner like her.

Besides, she was distracted by the cold seeping up from the floor and into her sit bones through her now-filthy sheath dress. She wouldn't have chosen winter white wool this morning had she known she'd be spending her day crawling through the woods and then sitting in a dank, subterranean cell. Yeah, meditation time was over.

Time to return to trying to figure out exactly where she was. Charlie had said the protestors were grabbed when it was dark out and were blindfolded for the trip back to the spot to be released. So he hadn't been able to provide any details. She, on the other hand, had the advantage of having grown up in Pittsburgh and being snatched off the street in broad daylight. She also had a phenomenally reliable internal clock.

So she knew that the trip from the spot where Vaughn Tabor had died to the cellar where she was being held had been a twenty-two-minute drive, exactly. There was, of course, no guarantee that the driver hadn't taken a roundabout route to prevent her from guessing where they were going. But given the current traffic snarls being caused by the fact that an entire bus had been swallowed by the earth in the middle of Grant Street, she was fairly confident that they had stayed on the East End of town. Otherwise, they'd still be sitting in traffic.

And they had definitely gone and stayed inside the Pittsburgh city limits after leaving Milltown. She could tell by the signage for the zoo and by the glimpse of the distinctive East Busway overhead as the van sped under the raised road. All signs pointed to her being held captive in the East Liberty/Shadyside/Bloomfield area—in other words, she was almost certainly within walking distance of her own home and office. This knowledge added Tantalus-like torture to her plight.

If she had to narrow it among the three, she'd guess East Liberty, based on the architecture she'd spied out the window. And the PPC did have headquarters in trendy Bakery Square, which was in the neighborhood. But this space wasn't part of anybody's urban revitalization plan, that much was certain. She was pretty sure she was being warehoused in an actual warehouse. Although she couldn't say for certain because the guy she'd kneecapped had eventually barked out an order for the driver to pull over, then blindfolded her with three minutes left in the trip.

Eventually—but maybe not until she didn't come home for dinner—Connelly would realize she'd gone missing and track her phone. Assuming that her car hadn't been stolen or towed, the phone would lead him to the spot where she'd been abducted and then ... and then the trail would go cold. For most people. Presumably not for her G-man husband. Please, not for her husband.

She inhaled slowly, deeply, and then exhaled even more slowly, pausing for a moment at the end of the exhale before taking her next breath. The slower she could get her heart rate, the more likely she was to trick her central nervous system into believing that she wasn't in danger. That was the theory, at least. If she could convince herself that she was safe, she could stave off the flood of cortisol that would prevent her from thinking clearly.

Of course, her growling stomach was another constant interruption that hampered her ability to strategize. And that was one she couldn't fake her way through. It was well past lunchtime, and she was starting to get shaky. She needed some protein and some fat, and fast. It had gotten so bad that she was having olfactory hallucinations: she smelled cookies. Sweet, buttery cookies.

31

Charlie struck out at the library. Oh, the librarians knew who Sam was, but no one had seen him or had any ideas where Charlie should look for him. Dejected, he'd called Raquel, who met him for an early lunch at the pizza joint down the street.

After lunch, on a whim, really, he told her he wanted to pop back in to the library once more before they headed home. He thought the afternoon crowd might be more familiar with Sam's comings and goings. And he didn't want to have to admit to Sasha and Naya Andrews, the super-investigator, that his efforts had been a bust.

"Sure," Raquel agreed readily.

She browsed through the magazines in the

periodical reading room while he roamed through the library, canvassing the staff, volunteers, and patrons. It was a repeat of the morning. Nobody knew anything. He was starting to lose heart. Then he struck a vein of gold in the audiovisual room.

"Sam Blank? Sure, he's in here all the time," the floppy-haired teen behind the circulation desk told him.

Charlie glanced around at the rows of carrels that ringed the room, each with a DVD player, a monitor, and a set of oversized headphones.

"Are you sure? He's—"

"Deaf," the kid said. "Yeah, I know. Mr. Blank watches his movies with the closed captioning on."

"Oh, right. Of course." Charlie shook his head at his own cluelessness.

"But that's not why he comes here. For the movies, I mean."

"Oh? Then why does he come here?"

The kid abandoned the stack of DVDs that he'd been checking in and came out from behind the desk. "Come on, I'll show you."

He trotted off down a small hallway to the right of the desk and Charlie followed. They stopped in front of a glass-fronted room, and the kid pushed open the door. He stepped inside and flipped a light switch. Dim, soft light puddled down from the ceiling to illuminate several over-stuffed chairs and small sofas, many of which had fleece blankets draped over their backs. The room was cozy, dark, and warm. Charlie yawned.

The kid laughed. "I know, right? It's like the greatest nap room ever."

It was. "But what is it?"

"It used to be the audiovisual room. The idea was to make it comfy for our movie watchers, but it was a little *too* comfortable. People tended to drift off to sleep and miss their movies. So, we moved the carrels with the DVD players out to the big room. Now this room just sits empty. Nobody uses it much." He dropped his gaze to the floor. "Except for some of the guys."

This kid was so transparent he was see-through.

"So you let the homeless men hang out back here when you're working. They sleep?"

The kid turned out the light, pulled the door closed, and hurried back up the hall without meeting Charlie's gaze.

"Yeah, I'm not supposed to. But, you know, it's

getting cold out, and they're harmless—most of them. And they know if they get rowdy, I'll have to ask them to leave." He turned and gave Charlie a quick look. "But Mr. Blank never does. Get rowdy, I mean. He falls right to sleep no matter what's going on. I wake him up when my shift ends."

Charlie could tell there was more to the story. "Why? He can't stay here after you leave?"

"He used to. But one of the librarians found him asleep back there and started yelling for him to wake up and get out. She didn't realize he couldn't hear her, and she ended up calling the cops. It was ... a bad scene. So now I make sure he's awake before I leave".

"What's your name?"

"Mike Young."

"Mike, I can tell you're a good person. I'm a friend of Sam's. He's gonna stay with me for a while, but he left this morning and didn't come back." Charlie figured a partial truth was better than a whole lie.

"Okay?"

"I'm worried something might have happened to him. Have you seen him today?"

Mike shook his head no. "Sorry, I haven't."

"Well, if he comes in, ask him to borrow a phone and text me so I know he's safe, okay?" He scribbled his name and number on a call slip and handed it across the desk.

"Sure thing." Mike pocketed his number and returned to the pile of DVDs.

"Thanks."

He turned and made his way through the maze of rooms. He was almost to the periodical reading room when Mike came jogging up behind him out of breath.

"Mr. Robinson, Mr. Robinson!" he stage whispered.

"Yeah?"

"Sam didn't come in, but the minute you left, one of his buddies did. He's another regular."

"You think this guy knows where Sam is?"

"I know he does. I asked him."

Charlie's pulse quickened. He'd done it. He'd found Sam.

He tried to keep his excitement in check. "Great. Where is he?"

"The police station. Joe says he got arrested this morning."

32

L eo, Finn, Fiona, and Mocha were almost home from their trip to the playground when Leo's cell phone rang. They'd just stopped so the twins could jump in a pile of crimson and orange maple leaves, and Mocha was busy barking at squirrels.

He took the phone from his pocket and checked the display.

"Naya, what's up?"

Her voice crackled with urgency. "Where are you?"

"We're walking back from the Blue Slide. We stopped at the church on the corner to jump in some leaves and terrorize the local wildlife. Where are you?"

"I'm on your front porch. Do you think you could hurry the kids along?"

"Yeah. Do you wanna tell me what's going on?"

"When you get here."

She ended the call.

Leo frowned down at his phone, then slipped it back into his coat pocket. "Come on, dinosaurs. It's getting chilly. Let's get home and have some hot cocoa and a snack."

"Dinosaurs are like chickens, right?" Fiona asked.

"Mmm-hmm," he answered distractedly.

"That's what I thought. What do chickens eat, Finny?" Fiona asked.

"Eggs?" Finn ventured.

His sister burst into peals of laughter. "Noooo, that would make them camping bells, silly!"

Leo's mind was on the unusual call from Naya. But 'camping bells' caught his attention. He turned and studied Fiona for a moment, then chuckled. "You mean cannibals. Cannibals are animals that eat their own species."

"Hmph. Well, camping bells sounds better," she insisted.

He herded them home quickly by suggesting they see if they could reach the sidewalk square in front of their porch before he counted to one hundred. They did it with nineteen digits to spare. When they saw Naya and Jordana standing on the porch, they broke into excited squeals and clambered up the stairs ahead of him. He and Mocha followed at a more sedate pace.

When he reached the porch, he noted Naya's drawn, tight expression and the furrow between her eyes. She was worried about something.

She smoothed her forehead and greeted the kids with a broad smile and two warm hugs. "Hey, super twins, I need to borrow your dad for a bit, so Jordana came to hang out with you. What do you think of that?"

They cheered excitedly at the prospect of spending an unplanned afternoon with their favorite babysitter. Connelly handed Mocha's leash to Jordana.

"They need a snack. Apples and almond butter are probably your best bet."

"And hot cocoa!" Fiona reminded him.

"And hot cocoa."

"Got it. Do the pets need to be fed?" She bent and scratched Mocha behind her ears.

Leo shook his head. "Not until seven, assuming I'm not back before then. I guess if I'm not, you'll—." He trailed off as he realized he had no idea where he was going or when he'd be back.

"I'll make dinner. And we'll do baths and pjs, too, if it gets late."

"You're a lifesaver. But I'm sure Sasha will be home before bedtime even if I'm not."

Jordana and Naya exchanged a furtive look. It was quick and subtle, and most people would have missed it. But he didn't, and something about it chilled him.

He crouched and gave Fiona and Finn each a hug and a kiss. "I love you. Be good for Jordana, please."

"We're always good," Finn said indignantly.

"Right, Jordana?" Fiona demanded.

Jordana grinned and winked broadly at the kids. "That's my story, and I'm sticking to it." She pulled out her set of keys, unlocked the door, and ushered them inside with promises of hot chocolate with marshmallows.

Leo turned to Naya. "Okay, now tell me what this is about."

Naya studied him for a long moment. "Have you heard from Sasha lately?"

He pulled out his cell phone and checked his text and call logs. "Not since early this morning. She was on her way to meet Charlie Robinson, and I texted her a picture of the kids. It was a little before eight o'clock. Why? What's going on?"

Naya frowned. "That's what I was afraid of. Look, do you want to drive or do you want me to?"

He glanced up and down the street but saw no sign of her BMW. "Where's your car?"

"We walked over, so we'll have to go back to the office to get it if you want me to drive."

"I'll drive then." He shrugged and headed for his SUV, which was parked in the driveway. "But you need to start talking, and I need to know where we're going."

She fell into step beside him and pulled out her own phone. "Your office. I already spoke to Hank. He's expecting us."

"Naya, for the last time, what's going on?"

He was starting to feel impatient. He popped

the locks and opened the passenger door for her, then circled the front of the SUV, trying to keep his irritation in check. As soon as he slid into the driver's seat, she turned to him and locked eyes with him.

"After Sasha met with Charlie, the two of them went to see Max Barefoot to get him to join in the complaint. According to Charlie, Landon Lewis had a team of men stationed outside Barefoot's house doing surveillance. Sasha made them and confronted them."

"That sounds like her."

"Yeah, it does. She told the guys on surveillance that she wanted Landon Lewis to contact her. Then she dropped Charlie off at the library to see if he could get a lead on Sam Blank's whereabouts."

"Wait, Blank? The deaf man? I thought he was staying with Charlie Robinson?"

"The imperative word in that sentence is *was*. Something spooked him, and he left. He was gone when Charlie woke up this morning. Mr. Barefoot suggested they check at the library for him. Sasha said she had something she needed to do and asked Charlie to look for Sam at the library. She gave him instructions to call me if he needed help, and then she texted me to let me know that. I got that text at ten-thirty. We exchanged a handful of texts then, but no one's heard from her since. She's not answering her cell phone. She's not returning texts or emails."

Leo pulled out and headed toward the field office, even though he thought Naya was perhaps overreacting, just slightly. "Maybe she's in court or at the training studio with Daniel—somewhere where she's not able to check her messages?"

Naya glared at him, eyes blazing. "Do you think I showed up at your house without asking Caroline to check her court calendar and appointment book first?" Her voice was heated.

"No, I guess not."

"That's right. And do you really think she's been sparring for the past five and a half hours?" She was still agitated, but her temper sprang from deep love and concern for Sasha.

He glanced at the clock. It was nearly four o'clock. That put Naya's concern into perspective.

"And you said nobody's heard from her since ten-thirty?"

"Yeah, and here's the thing, Leo—Charlie did find out where Sam Blank is."

"That's good news, right?"

"Well, it's good that we know where he is. It's bad that he's been re-arrested by the Milltown police. Charlie texted that to Sasha at one-thirty. No response. There's zero chance your wife would ignore a text telling her her client was in custody. None."

Leo's calm facade began to slip. "No, you're right. She wouldn't. Maybe she's at the police station. Maybe she found out before Charlie did. Maybe Sam called her. Maybe—"

"Maybe so. I hope you're right. But since nobody's heard from her ..."

Realization dawned. "You want me and Hank to track her phone."

"It's an emergency."

"I promised her I wouldn't ever do that, Naya. After Tannerville—"

"I know you did. And, believe me, I know how she feels about it. Big Brother, creepy surveillance state, invasion of privacy, infantilizing. Trust me. I've heard the speech."

"And you still want to do it?"

She turned and looked him full in the face. "Leo, I have a really bad feeling."

His stomach hit his shoes. "Then we'll do it."

"Good. Maybe you could drive a little faster?"

He threw her a look but hit the gas. He used his voice assistant to dictate a text to Sasha as he zoomed through a light that was definitely no longer yellow. "Text Sasha's mobile: if you get this, ping me. Love, L. Send text."

Naya watched out of the corner of her eye but didn't comment. He was glad for that. He didn't want to talk about his rising worry.

After a beat, he asked, "Did Charlie know why they arrested Sam again?"

"No." She hesitated. "But you know what he saw, right?"

"Yeah, I know," he answered grimly. They drove in silence the rest of the way.

33

L andon hummed a Christmas carol as he walked into the conference room. He saw no reason to subject Ms. McCandless-Connelly to the box. He could afford to be civilized with her.

His tune died in his throat when he pushed open the door and got a look at her. Her expensive cream-colored suit dress was streaked with dirt and blood, and her hair hung over her face like a curtain. She raised her chin when the door opened and pinned him with glittering green eyes that looked out from a face that was covered in scratches. A red bruise on her puffy left cheekbone was already darkening to purple.

He grimaced, then pasted on a smile and

strode across the room, his hand outstretched. "Ms. McCandless-Connelly, I'm Landon Lewis."

She didn't accept his handshake, and he blinked at the affront. After a moment, she snorted and half-stood from the chair and raised her shoulders. Chains rattled. She was cuffed and shackled to a waist belt.

"I can't shake. Not that I would."

"Oh, for heaven's sake, take those off," he ordered Agent Scott.

Scott and Fox exchanged a look.

Fox cleared his throat. "Sir, the team who picked her up said she's violent."

"Agent Fox, *look* at her. She's the size of a small middle school child or maybe a large fifth grader. She can't weigh a hundred pounds. Moreover, Cesare has determined she's absolutely no threat. Zero latent criminality." He shook his head.

"Sir—"

"*Now,* agent."

"You're the boss." Scott, who was closer to her, shrugged and bent to unlock the cuffs, then the shackles, and finally removed the length of chain.

"Thank you," Sasha said.

"You're quite welcome. And I apologize for the rough treatment. It appears to have been considerable overkill," Landon told her.

"Do you think I could get a cup of coffee? It's been a long day." She smiled warmly.

"Of course." He turned to the guards. "Bring us coffee service, please."

Fox raised an eyebrow, then nodded. The pair left the room. Landon considered the woman for a long moment, trying to ascertain how to approach her. Directly, he decided.

"I understand your services have been engaged by Messrs. Blank and Barefoot and Professor Robinson."

"Yes. We plan to sue the Milltown Police Department and Chief Carlson, personally, for various violations of my clients' civil rights."

"I see. So why are you seeking copies of the nondisclosure agreements your clients signed with my company? We're not part of the police department."

"No, Mr. Lewis, you're not. The Milltown Police Department, whatever flaws it might have, is an official law enforcement organization, subject to state and federal oversight. Your PPC

Program is rogue, secret, unaccountable, and unsupervised."

"Are you saying you intend to sue the PPC, as well?"

"Yes," she said evenly.

He pressed his palms against the table and held her unwavering gaze. "I wish you wouldn't. Perhaps you don't understand what it is we do here."

The door opened, and Fox entered the room with a coffee tray and a surly expression. Landon ignored the scowl. "Thank you, agent."

The guard slammed the tray down on the table with unnecessary force, turned on his heel, and stomped out of the room. Landon rolled his eyes. He poured coffee from the carafe into two blue ceramic mugs and placed one in front of the lawyer. She picked it up and cupped her hands around it as if it were precious.

"Cream and sugar?" he offered.

"Black is fine, thanks."

He stirred cream and sugar into his own mug until the coffee was the perfect shade of pale tan. "I wish he'd thought to bring some cookies," he mused.

She blinked. "Did you say cookies?"

"Yes, why?"

"I've been smelling cookies—butter cookies —for hours in that cell. I thought I was imagining it."

He chuckled. "No, the cookies are quite real. This space used to house a test kitchen for the Nabisco Company—not the manufacturing plant proper."

She sipped her coffee. "Right, because that's been turned into retail space and a hotel."

"Correct. We're sitting in a warehouse about a quarter of a mile away. Above ground, I have my headquarters. Down here, we use this basement space as a beta test for our detention program."

"And where do the cookies come in?"

"Oh, right. When we bought the space, the contents conveyed. And those contents included several hundred pounds of cookie dough in a deep freezer, along with the commercial ovens in which to bake them. So, we indulge in the occasional treat."

"Interesting." She took another drink.

"It is, if one's a history buff. I'm more of a futurist, personally." He steered their conversation back to the topic at hand.

She took the bait. "And Cesare is the criminologist of the future, right?"

He frowned at her tone. "You seem to think it's not."

"I think your AI is wrong more often than not. It's not even as accurate as a coin flip."

"That's false. It's patently untrue." He struggled to keep his temper as she smiled at him, catlike, over the coffee mug.

"Isn't it? Charlie Robinson's not a latent criminal. And Sam Blank? Please."

"Don't lay Sam Blank at my feet. Milltown wanted him to be picked up, not me."

Her satisfied expression made him wonder if she'd taken the bait or if he had. "What about Max Barefoot—do you stand by Cesare's assessment of him?"

"Mr. Barefoot is a felon. His childhood and educational background combined with his criminal record led Cesare to—"

"Mr. Barefoot is a homeowner. A taxpayer. And a Black man. Isn't that what this is really about?"

"Cesare is a series of ones and zeros. As I explained to Professor Robinson, it can't be racist."

"No. But you can. And you programmed it. These men who you say are latent criminals. They all remind you of your son's killer, don't they? They're big and scary and Black. Like Calvin Tennyson. But me? I'm a small White woman. I'm harmless. Right?"

He blanched at her mention of Josh and his murderer. "How dare you dredge up my personal pain to use against me."

"Says the kidnapper," she snickered. She waited a beat, as if he was supposed to rethink his life choices, then she went on. "I know how you feel, believe it or not. My brother was shot and killed when I was nineteen. Twenty years ago yesterday, as a matter of fact. I've felt that pain. But your attempts to manage it and control it aren't working, Mr. Lewis. All of this isn't keeping anyone safe or honoring his memory. It's just keeping you tethered to the pain of the past." She waved her empty coffee mug around the room in a sweeping gesture that encompassed the building.

"You're wrong."

"No. You're wrong."

She slammed the mug down hard on the edge of the table. It smashed apart, and before he'd even reacted to the crashing sound, she was on her feet, running at him. And then, somehow, she had a clump of his hair in her right hand, pulling his head back and exposing his neck. With her left, she pressed a sharp shard of the ceramic mug against his bare skin. He swallowed, and the jagged edge dug into his right carotid artery.

"One slice, down and to the left, and you'll be bleeding out. So tell me again how I'm not a threat."

"What ... what do you want?" he managed.

"The truth."

34

Leo stood in front of Sasha's station wagon, stared down at the blinking dot on the GPS tracker app, and fought back a wave of nausea. Her car, her phone, and her bag were here on this windy stretch of road made famous by the image of a young man bleeding to death on the shoulder. But no Sasha.

It was as if she'd vanished into thin air. Or into the woods.

He turned. Hank and Naya were already at the edge of the lot, scanning the ground. He jogged over to join them.

"Find anything?"

Naya looked at Hank, expectant.

He cleared his throat. "Looks like there was a scuffle here in the gravel." He toed the ground where several semi-circles of pebbles were disturbed. "And see those tire tracks over there? I think she must've been ambushed."

Leo crouched and studied the ground. "That's blood, isn't it?" He pointed to a dark, wet clump of gravel.

Naya squatted beside him and rested a hand on his shoulder. "Could be. But, come on, Fly Boy, you know Sasha. Odds are it's not hers, it's theirs. His. Whoever's."

He nodded and blinked. "Right. I need some air."

He stood and walked into the brush, his back to his partner and Sasha's car, and filled his lungs with air so cold it burned.

Where was she? Who had her?

His mind raced, and he forced himself to stop the spiral. He looked out over the bare tops of trees, watching a vee of birds wing their way toward warmth. And then he spotted something colorful flapping against an oak tree in the distance. And he ran toward it.

When he reached the oak, he sagged against its trunk and made a guttural sound that felt like it was ripped from his chest. The bright fabric flapping in the wind was Sasha's scarf—a distinctive crimson, orange, and cream pattern—caught on a tree limb.

He unwound the scarf delicately, like he was performing surgery, and pressed his face into it to inhale his wife's spicy, gingery scent. Then he folded it carefully, lengthwise and then in half, and trudged back to the spot where Hank and Naya waited at the car, twin somber expressions on their tense faces.

"We need to mobilize a search party," he croaked, holding up the scarf. "She went into the woods."

Naya shook her head.

"She's not in the woods now, Leo," Hank said. He held up a small, round tracker. "This was attached to the undercarriage of her car. Someone followed her here and took her."

Leo gripped the soft fabric like a lifeline. "Someone. You mean Lewis."

"Probably," Naya said. "Hank thinks he can reverse triangulate the location, isolate the tracking software, lead us to Lewis or whoever's got her, wherever they are."

"To hell with that. We're going to his headquarters, and I'm going to shake it out of him if I have to," he growled.

"That works, too," Hank agreed.

35

Sasha clenched her fist in Landon Lewis' over-gelled hair and hissed in his ear. "What happened to Vaughn Tabor? Why are the Milltown Police so interested in Sam Blank?"

He tented his eyebrows and tried to turn to look at her. She pressed the sharp point of the ceramic mug handle into his throat. He froze.

"I ... I don't know why they want Mr. Blank so badly, but ... Vaughn Tabor was shot during an altercation with the police. Everybody knows that."

For an evil super-genius, this guy was dense. She didn't have time to pull the answers out of him one word at a time. His goon squad would eventually come back to see if he wanted more coffee, and when they found her holding a weapon to his throat, they were unlikely to underreact.

"Yes, Landon. Everybody knows that. And Sam Blank knows what really happened, because he saw it. So. What. Did. He. See?" She spat the words and punctuated each syllable with a jab of the broken piece of mug.

He whimpered. "Sam Blank was there the night Tabor was shot?"

"Are you telling me you didn't know?"

He started to shake his head, then remembered the improvised knife at his throat and stopped. "I swear, I didn't."

She laughed a mirthless laugh. "You've been played by a rinky-dink local police station, you and your sophisticated predictive and preventive crime program. That's priceless."

His face clouded. "They're not so rinky-dink after all, I think."

She frowned. Now what was he on about?

Before she could ask, she heard shouting and heavy feet running down the hall.

Crap, here comes Landon's cavalry.

She jerked him to his feet, tightened her left

elbow around his neck, and yanked him away from the table, backing them up against the far wall. She positioned him in front of her, just in case the goon squad burst in, guns blazing— which frankly struck her as exactly the sort of dramatic overkill that crew would go for.

The door flew open. She was about to find out.

But the men who ran in weren't Landon's thugs. Her husband raced through the door with Hank Richardson on his heels. The sight of Connelly and his partner flooded her with relief and love and an overwhelming desire to throw herself into Connelly's arms and bury her face into his broad chest. Although, in fairness, they *did* have their guns drawn. The heartfelt reunion would have to wait until they dealt with Landon Lewis and his army of giants.

Naya trailed them into the room, nibbling on a cookie.

"Are you eating sugar?" Sasha blurted.

Naya shrugged. "Exigent circumstances. Carl will understand."

Then the shouting started.

36

Leo didn't know whether he wanted to laugh or cry at the sight of his filthy, bruised, and battered wife holding the mastermind behind the PPC program hostage with a chunk of a broken coffee mug. He didn't have time to do much more than give her a lopsided grin before a squadron of guards or agents or whatever these people were rushed into the room yelling orders and brandishing their weapons.

The situation had suddenly become incredibly dangerous. The five men in black were all armed with assault rifles. Leo and Hank had a Sig Sauer and a Glock, respectively. Naya was packing a sugar cookie, and Sasha had her ceramic shard. Lewis looked like he was about to vomit.

"Stand down," Leo shouted at the guards. He barked the order in his loudest, most forceful voice. "I'm Special Agent Connelly. This is Special Agent-in-Charge and Director Richardson. We're operating under the authority of the Department of Homeland Security. Stand down." It was mostly true.

He trained his gun on the closest man while Hank reached into his hip pocket and pulled out one of the badges the two of them used to impersonate agents from other departments. It did the trick. The men were clearly well disciplined. Former military or government or law enforcement of some kind, Leo surmised. They lowered their weapons without hesitation and stood at attention. Landon Lewis sagged and seemed to shrink in Sasha's grip.

Naya finished her cookie and dusted the crumbs from her fingertips.

"You okay, Mac?" she asked Sasha.

Sasha smiled, "Better now."

Leo studied her face. When he found out which one of these thugs had given her the bruise that was blooming on her cheekbone, they'd regret it.

Lewis cleared his throat. "Director Richardson, there must be some misunderstanding. This operation is authorized at the highest levels."

Hank scoffed. "Nice try. Your beta program gets funding under a grant. And yeah, the powers that be look the other way while you run your little experiment because, of course, they'd love to be able to prevent crimes by predicting them before they happen. Wouldn't we all? But this isn't a science fiction movie. This is real life. And you're holding a civilian, a scrap of a woman, without authorization."

Lewis blanched and protested. "To the contrary, this woman is holding me against my will. I mean, look at her. I intend to press charges."

Hank raised one eyebrow. "You look at her. She's obviously been beaten. And she happens to be integral to an operation that supersedes your program. You'll be releasing her into our custody, and you most certainly will not be pressing charges. She might be, though. And, of course, there will be consequences for interfering with an active DHS operation."

Lewis blanched and began to stammer.

Naya spoke over him. "Listen, can you all do the penis-measuring part later? Don't forget, Sam's cooling his heels at the Milltown police station without the benefit of an interpreter or a lawyer."

Sasha snapped her eyes from Leo's face to Naya's. "They arrested Sam?"

Naya nodded. "Yeah, Will's on his way over there with Charlie. But *you're* Sam's lawyer. We should get over there."

Sasha hesitated. "What do we do with these guys?"

Hank said, "Cole's home. He's watching the rest of the kids for me. So I'll babysit this crew. But you should take Lewis with you—in case you need leverage with the police."

"Thanks, Hank."

"Of course. Don't mention it. Go," he urged.

She turned to Leo. "Speaking of kids, where are ours?"

"Jordana's with them."

Lewis piped up. "Wait. You have children together? Connelly, McCandless-Connelly. You're married?"

Leo didn't bother to respond. Instead, he

plucked a set of handcuffs from the closest guard and barked, "Key!"

The man slapped the key to the cuffs into Leo's palm. Leo advanced on Lewis. Then his attention shifted to Sasha. He gingerly brushed her swollen cheekbone with his fingertips. "Does it hurt?"

She smiled crookedly. "You should see the other guy."

"I think I already did. I assume he's the one with the bandaged knee and the crutches who's sitting at the front desk?"

"Yeah, that's him."

He shook his head. "You really scared me."

"I really scared me, too. And I need to rethink my footwear. But we can do this part later, okay? When we don't have an audience." She jerked her head toward Lewis.

"Definitely. You can let go of him now."

She dropped the jagged piece of ceramic to the floor and gave Lewis a small shove toward Leo. Leo clamped the cuffs on his wrists and tightened them—possibly more than was strictly necessary. He grabbed Lewis by the arm and marched him toward the door.

Sasha stopped to give Hank a quick hug.

"Thank you. But, really, scrap of a woman? We're going to have words later."

He grinned, then nodded. "Go."

As Leo, Sasha and Naya headed for the door with Landon in tow, Hank called after Naya, "Hey, where'd you get those cookies?"

"The men in black have a sweet break room. I'm sure one of your new friends will be happy to fix you a plate," she said over her shoulder.

The door swung closed behind them, and they hustled Landon through the maze of halls and out into the parking lot.

37

Sasha, Connelly, and Naya hurried inside the police station, brushing the snowflakes from their shoulders and stamping their feet and ignoring Landon's litany of complaints. Will and Charlie looked up from the wooden bench where they waited.

"You look like hell," Will said by way of greeting.

Sasha laughed. She felt like hell, too.

"Thanks, Will. You know how to make a girl feel good. What's the story with Sam?" She nodded to include Charlie in the question.

Will frowned. "They haven't let us back to see him. He hasn't been charged, so he's not entitled to a lawyer yet."

"It's after seven. What time did they pick him up?" she asked.

"He's been here since this morning," Charlie said, agitated. "Without any way to communicate with anybody."

Will put a calming hand on Charlie's arm. "It's wrong. There's no question that it's wrong, but keep this in mind: if he can't communicate with them, they also can't communicate with him. So they're not asking any questions. That's good, at least."

Connelly wrinkled his forehead. "I don't understand the endgame here. What's their plan? If they're not questioning him, and they're not charging him, why is he here?"

"That's the million-dollar question," Will agreed.

Sasha scanned the small lobby. "Who's on duty?"

"Paul Holtzman is stationed at the front desk. World's Greatest Dad mug. Takes his coffee with cinnamon on your recommendation."

Landon Lewis piped up, "Is Chief Carlson here?"

"What's he doing here?" Charlie demanded as if he only just noticed his former tormentor.

"We brought him in case we need him for leverage."

"Leverage over whom?"

"Over the dirty cops scuttling around this building like roaches."

Charlie snorted. "Wouldn't that be all of them?"

"We're going to need to find some allies in this building," Connelly said in a soft voice. "It'd be helpful if you could keep your personal opinions to yourself until we get Sam out of here."

Charlie's eyes flashed, but he nodded. "Got it."

"Thanks," Connelly said. "By the way, I'm Leo Connelly. Sasha's husband."

"Charlie Robinson."

"Is Kara Diamond on duty?" Lewis asked.

Sasha turned to Lewis and hissed, "Nobody wants to hear from you."

"That may be, but I think Officer Diamond is part of the effort to silence Mr. Blank."

Sasha wheeled around. "Based on what?"

"She told me that Officer Willard flagged Sam Blank for detention when they were reviewing the facial recognition software on the traffic camera during the protest. But Holtzman said it wasn't Willard, Officer Comford was the one who insisted he be picked up."

"So, how do you know Holtzman's not lying?" Connelly demanded.

"Just a hunch, I guess. I spoke to Officers Diamond and Comford the other night. There was an ... undercurrent."

Sasha pursed her lips and decided not to say what she thought of Lewis' judgment. From the look on Connelly's face, he shared her opinion.

"Is Diamond here?" Lewis repeated.

Will looked at Charlie, and they both shrugged.

"I saw a female officer walk through a while ago, but I don't know her name," Will finally answered.

"Is she an older woman with short-cropped gray hair?" Sasha asked.

He shook his head. "Nope. Young, long dark hair in a ponytail."

"That's Brittany Comford," Lewis volunteered.

"We're not going to stand out here all night," Connelly said. "I'm going to find somebody to ask."

Will held up a hand to stop him. "I don't

think we should go back there uninvited, Leo."

"I have a calling card." He wrenched Lewis by the arm and darted behind the desk.

Sasha shot a look at Naya. "You three hang tight. We'll be right back." She raced off after her husband and Lewis.

"Hey, is anybody here?" Connelly bellowed. "I want to report a crime. A man's been abducted."

"What are you doing?"

"I'm tired of this. I want to be done with this. I want to get Sam Blank out of here, then have you checked out to make sure your cheekbone's not shattered."

"It's not."

"Last time I checked, you're not a doctor. And I want to go home and play with our kids. In short, I'm not interested in diplomacy; I'm interested in efficiency."

Sasha sighed. This was a side that her even-tempered husband rarely displayed. But she knew from experience that when he did, there was no point in trying to cajole him out of it.

Apparently roused by Connelly's yelling, two uniformed police officers came running up the hallway.

Holtzman was in the lead, followed by a dark-haired woman.

"Stop!" Officer Holtzman commanded.

Sasha raised her hands and waved them to show they were empty. "Officer, we met the other night when I came to get Jordana Morgan after the protest. I'm an attorney. I'm not armed."

Holtzman squinted at her. "Hey, cinnamon coffee."

She smiled. "That's me. And you know Mr. Lewis."

Holtzman's eyes shifted. He took in the handcuffs around Lewis' wrists and squared shoulders. "Mr. Lewis, what's going on here? Is everything all right?"

Lewis didn't respond at first. So Connelly gave him a shake and jolted an answer loose.

"This gentleman is a federal agent. Apparently, my program got mixed up with one of his operations, and there's some question about which one takes precedence. We'll get it sorted. I think, at the moment, his priority is finding Mr. Blank." Lewis pitched his version smoothly, the consummate salesman.

Holtzman cut his eyes toward the dark-haired woman behind him. "Officers Comford and

Diamond picked him up this morning. He's part of an active investigation. It has nothing to do with the protest, and I'm sure it has nothing to do with this federal operation you mentioned." Behind him, Comford nodded.

Lewis leaned toward Sasha. "*Psst.*"

She gave him a sidelong glance. "What?"

He tilted his head in the universal 'come here' gesture. She raised an eyebrow but leaned over.

"Comford's the duty officer who was here the other night. She's skittish."

"What do you mean by skittish?"

"She has an itchy trigger finger."

Connelly turned and glared at Lewis, who clamped his mouth shut. Sasha laced her fingers together, stretched her arms in front of her, and thought for a moment. She played it out in her mind.

Then she locked eyes with Officer Holtzman. "Officer Comford was one of the officers who responded to the disturbance call near the bypass, right? She shot Vaughn Tabor."

Behind Holtzman, Comford stiffened and glanced involuntarily at the interview room to her left.

Sasha pointed at the door. "Is Mr. Blank in that room?"

Holtzman nodded.

"And Kara Diamond's in there with him?"

"Correct."

"She's protecting you, isn't she?" Sasha addressed the woman behind Paul Holtzman.

"I don't know what you're talking about," the officer stammered.

"Really? You panicked in the field and shot an unarmed civilian. She's trying to help you clean it up. It's not rocket science. I just want to know if this is some sisters in blue BS."

"Clean what up?" Holtzman demanded.

"Sam Blank was in the woods that night. He saw what happened. He saw her shoot Vaughn Tabor. And without knowing any of the details of the DA's investigation, I'll bet Sam saw her or Diamond plant a weapon on the body. *That's* why they're so dead set on arresting Sam."

Comford drew her weapon and aimed at Landon Lewis. "She's lying. She's lying, and your program screwed up. Sam Blank is a homeless degenerate. He's exposed himself. He's got vagrancy and trespassing complaints. And your useless AI program didn't flag him. This is your fault." Her hand trembled.

Connelly noticed, too. He pulled his gun from his shoulder holster and leveled it at Comford. Holtzman rested his hand on the butt of his gun.

Sasha had a vision of a shootout like the ones in the black-and-white cowboy movies her grandfather used to watch. "Hold on. Everybody just calm down," she said in the voice she used when Fiona or Finn started to spiral out of control. "Let's just take a breath and talk about this."

Holtzman's fingers relaxed, and Connelly lowered his weapon. Comford was still shaking, but she nodded and holstered her gun, too.

Sasha exhaled, a wave of relief crashing over her. And that's when the interview room door swung open to reveal Kara Diamond standing in the doorway in a classic shooting stance with her weapon drawn.

"Comford's right, you know, Landon. All you needed to do was identify Blank as a danger. Then we could've kept them in detention indefinitely. This is your fault."

Diamond's finger twitched, and Sasha didn't

have time to think. She dove at Landon, pushing him hard. He landed on the floor with a thud, and she threw herself on top of him as the bullet tore through the air above their heads and pierced the wall.

Holtzman turned and started shouting at Diamond. "Drop it, drop it!"

She engaged the safety and placed the gun on the floor.

"Kick it over here!"

She did. Holtzman picked up the weapon one-fingered, and Connelly covered Comford while Paul Holtzman handcuffed his direct superior. Then, ashen-faced, he took Comford's service piece and cuffed her, as well.

Connelly crouched beside Sasha. "Are you hurt?"

She shook her head no. Her heart was thumping too fast. She couldn't speak. He helped her to her feet.

"What about him?" she managed, nodding toward Lewis, who was curled into the fetal position, shaking. "You could probably uncuff him now."

He returned to the floor and worked the key to release the handcuffs.

"Thank you," Lewis said as he made his way to his feet and dusted off his suit.

"Don't thank me, thank Sasha. I probably would've let Diamond shoot you, personally."

Lewis studied Sasha gravely. "Thank you." After a moment, he said, "This is going to be an unholy mess. Everyone's going to sue everyone, and PPC is going to have to lawyer up. So I'll deny saying this later, but Cesare was never intended to be used this way."

She was about to tell him all about good intentions and how the roads to hell are paved. Before she had the chance, Will, Charlie, and Naya ran in from the lobby.

"Is everybody okay?" Naya asked.

Connelly nodded.

"Who fired their weapon?" Will wanted to know.

"Officer Diamond," Connelly answered. "She tried to take out Lewis. Sasha probably saved his life."

She smiled weakly. "Will, could you and Charlie go get Sam. He's in that interview room." She turned toward Holtzman. "I assume you're going to release him into our custody?"

He nodded briskly.

38

Friday, November 22, 2019
mid-afternoon

Sasha mounted the steps to the library slowly, rehearsing what she planned to say. The campus was mostly deserted, with most of the students scattered to their hometowns for the upcoming Thanksgiving break. And the library was no exception. The clack of her shoes striking the highly polished floor echoed in the cavernous empty building. There were no students at the gleaming chestnut tables. No students sitting at the carrels ringing the perimeter of the study space. The place was a ghost town.

She approached the circulation desk.

"Can I help you?" Patrick's son asked.

She stared at him for a long moment.

"Ma'am?" he gave her a puzzled look.

Lord, but he looked like Patrick.

She caught her lower lip between her teeth, then she exhaled shakily. "Are you Matthew MacManus?" She wondered if he heard the tremor in her voice.

He nodded. "I'm sorry, do I know you?"

"No. Not yet."

He frowned uneasily. "I don't understand." He shifted his weight from one foot to the other.

She plunged forward. "I'm your aunt. My name's Sasha McCandless-Connelly."

He shook his head. "No, my parents are both only children. You must have me confused with somebody else."

"Your mom, Allie, was my college roommate my freshman and sophomore years. My older brother Patrick had a relationship with her. You're my brother's son."

His nostrils flared and his color rose. "Look,

lady, I'm not sure what's going on here, but my dad's name is Devon MacManus."

She reached into her bag and took out the newspaper clipping of Patrick at the state baseball championship. She rested it on the desk. "No, Matthew. Your dad's name was Patrick McCandless. He died twenty years ago, when your mom was pregnant with you. Look." She tapped the picture.

"You need to leave. I'll call security."

"I'm going. My business card's clipped to the article. You should call your mom and ask her if I'm telling the truth. I also wrote your grandparents' address on my card. If you're staying in town for Thanksgiving, you're welcome to join us for dinner on Thursday. We eat at six."

She turned and walked out of the library, her legs shaking. When she reached the car, she sank into the passenger seat and closed her eyes.

Connelly looked over at her. "How'd it go?"

"I don't know yet."

"But you did it."

"I did it."

He leaned across the console and kissed her gently. She kissed him back with an urgency that surprised her.

He started the engine. "Do you want me to drop you at work?"

"How long did my parents say they could keep the kids?"

"As long as we want. They're helping grandma make a cornucopia for the centerpiece next week."

A slow smile spread across her face. "In that case, why don't we go back to the house."

"In the middle of the workday, Ms. McCand-less-Connelly?"

"The work'll still be there on Monday. I mean, unless you have somewhere else you'd rather be?"

In response, he gunned the engine and zipped out of the parking spot.

She called into the office on the way back to the house to check messages.

Caroline read her a list of calls that could definitely wait to be returned until after she and Connelly had taken advantage of the empty house.

"Oh, and the copy service called," Caroline added.

"Okay?"

"They need prior authorization to pull the

files Naya requested from the court docket. They're billed to the pro bono number, and you're listed as the responsible attorney."

"Go ahead and authorize it."

"There are *a lot* of files."

"It's fine," Sasha assured her.

"Okay," Caroline said dubiously. "Are e-copies okay?"

Sasha groaned inwardly. "Let's splurge on hard copies."

"You need to get your vision checked again," Caroline mother-henned her.

"Duly noted."

Sasha ended the call as Connelly pulled into the driveway and gave her *that look.* Thoughts of reading glasses and court motions fell out of her head entirely.

39

Tuesday, November 26, 2019

Sasha was reviewing her statement for Milltown's hastily created Civilian Review Board when Naya knocked lightly on her door and pushed it open.

"Special delivery," she sing-songed as she walked into the room with an armload of files.

"Wait, what's all this?"

Naya dumped the mountain of files on the corner of Sasha's desk. "Did you or did you not request copies of all cases filed by the Milltown District Attorney in the past ten years in which the prosecution moved to admit evidence under the inevitable discovery exception to the exclusionary rule?"

She stared at the thick pile of folders. "All of these?"

"Oh, no. This is just the tip of the iceberg." Naya leaned out into the hallway and called, "Bring them in, Jordana."

Jordana wheeled in a hand truck loaded down with Bankers boxes and parked it in the middle of the office. "Why did you order hard copies? You know you could've just had them imaged, right?"

"Ask me again when you're about to turn forty. The print just keeps getting smaller." Sasha told her.

She gaped at the boxes then narrowed her eyes at Naya. "Is this your idea of a joke?"

Naya shook her head. "Sorry, Mac. Careful what you wish for, I guess. I know what you're doing over the holiday weekend."

"The holiday weekend? More like, until the twins graduate high school. This is unreal. So, they just violated the Fourth Amendment willy-nilly." She shook her head at the tower of boxes.

"I'll help you," Jordana offered. "It's the least I

can do for the woman who's bringing Vaughn Tabor's killer to justice."

Sasha surveyed the boxes. "I don't even know what to say."

Naya laughed. "You better say yes before she comes to her senses. What's going on with Lewis and the PPC?"

"He's entering into a consent decree with the Justice Department. He's agreed to mothball the PPC. But he still thinks Cesare is viable AI. Now he wants to use it to weed out bad cops."

Naya studied her. "You don't think that's a better use for it?"

"No, I don't. Any program, even one capable of learning, has to be created by a human who has human biases. We understand that people are biased, but we expect machines to be impartial. It's too dangerous. I think Lewis had good intentions. It's just a terrible idea."

"But we should be weeding out dirty cops," Jordana protested.

"I agree. And we should be preventing crimes. But an algorithm isn't the way to do it," Sasha said. "It'd be as wrong to make those determinations about law enforcement officers as it was to make them about so-called latent criminals. You can't pre-judge people that way, Jordana. Or, at least you shouldn't."

Jordana looked doubtful. "I'm not sure I agree."

"And that's fine. You don't have to. But if you're really willing to help me dig through these files. I'd appreciate the help. If they show what I think they're going to show, the Vaughn Tabor shooting and the attempt to railroad Sam Blank are literally only the very beginning of the story. I think the Milltown PD has been slowly rotting from the inside for a *long* time."

"Gee, I'd offer to give the two of you a hand, but I talked Carl into a getaway. We're going down to the Outer Banks next week for a little out of season beach trip," Naya said in a tone that screamed *sorry, not sorry.*

"A whole week under Carl's watchful eye. How are you going to sneak your sugar?"

Naya gave her a look. "Please. As if I didn't already think about that. The house I rented is directly across the street from a Duck Donuts. I'm going to be taking a lot of walks."

Sasha smiled.

"What?"

"Nothing. Sounds like a plan."

Carl had confided to Connelly that he knew Naya was still indulging in sugar. As long as she kept pretending she wasn't, he was going to make her jump through the hoops. Sasha wasn't sure who was getting over on whom at this point.

"Do you have plans for Thanksgiving?" Jordana asked Sasha.

"We'll go to my parents' place."

"Will all your relatives be there?"

Would they?

"Maybe."

"Nice. I'm boycotting the holiday. My mom's ticked, but I can't celebrate what the Pilgrims did to the indigenous peoples," Jordana explained. "Maybe I'll get a jump start on those files while you're stuffing your faces with turkey."

"Have at it, my friend," Sasha responded.

40

Thursday, November 28, 2019
Thanksgiving Day

Sasha's parents' house was full of people, food, and noise. Her dad and brothers were gathered around the television in the living room watching the football game. Connelly and the older kids were playing a game of Clue in the den. And her sisters-in-law and mom were bustling around the kitchen. She felt a little lost.

She wandered into the sunroom where

Daniella, Julian, and the twins were making felt turkeys. She watched for a bit as Daniella tried to help the little ones with the scissors. Predictably, Fiona rejected any assistance and had the crooked, but independently created, turkey to show for it.

"Hi, Aunt Sasha," Daniella chirped.

"Hi, kiddo. Your mom told me you're a vegan."

"Uh-huh?" She looked up with concern, as if maybe Sasha was going to mock her nascent rebellion.

"Well, I made a dessert especially for you. It's a vegan pumpkin cheesecake."

Her eyes shined. "You did? For me?"

"Yep."

Finn and Fiona exchanged a look. She knew what they were thinking. She didn't do a lot of baking, and it hardly seemed fair that she'd made something special for their cousin, but not for them.

"We're vegans, too," Finn informed her.

"Oh, really? Well, it's a pretty big cheesecake. I think there's plenty for everyone. *And* I baked a pumpkin pie for anybody who isn't a vegan."

Satisfied, the twins returned to their turkeys. Sasha made her way to the kitchen to see if she could lend a hand. As usual, her mother, Riley, and Jordan shooed her away from the stove and suggested she set the table. Fine by her. She was folding linen napkins in the dining room when the doorbell rang.

Her mom poked her head out from the kitchen.

"Did I just hear the door? Everybody's here."

Sasha shrugged and kept folding napkins. A moment later, the doorbell rang again. She sighed and abandoned the stack of linens.

"Really?" She nudged Sean as she walked through the living room. "Nobody else can hear the door?"

Her brothers and father didn't acknowledge her. In fact, their attention never wavered from the television. She stalked to the front of the house and yanked the door open.

Matthew MacManus stared at her wide-eyed, gripping a bouquet of fall flowers. "Um ... am I still invited?"

"Sure, of course. Come in," she stammered as she ushered him into the house. "Can I take your coat?"

He wriggled out of his navy peacoat while she held his bouquet. Then she handed the flowers back to him and took his coat. After she hung it in the hall coat closet, she led Matthew into the living room.

"Dad, mute that for a second, okay?"

Her father turned to frown at her and caught sight of the teenager standing next to her. His mouth fell open for a moment. Then he cleared his throat and popped to his feet, still staring at Matthew.

He called out to the kitchen, "Val, could you come in here, please?"

Sasha's mom walked into the room, wiping her hands on her apron. "Pat, what is it? I'm busy."

She stopped in the doorway and gasped, covering her mouth with her hand. Ryan and Sean finally turned around. Ryan grabbed the remote and clicked the television off.

"Mom, Dad, Sean, Ryan, this is Matthew. Matthew, these are your uncles and your grandparents."

Sasha's mom crossed herself.

"You look exactly like him," Sean said thickly, getting to his feet.

There was a long, awkward pause that stretched on until Daniella and the twins came running in from the sunroom to show off their crafts. They screeched to a halt and gawked at Matthew.

"Who are you?" Finn demanded.

"This is your cousin, Matthew," Sasha's mom explained.

Finn gave her a skeptical look. Fiona tugged on his arm and whispered in his ear. Sasha thought she caught the phrase *'fancy manners.'* He nodded, then stuck out his hand.

"I'm Finn Connelly. This is my sister Fiona. I'm pleased to meet you."

Matthew laughed and crouched down to shake hands with Finn. "The pleasure is all mine."

"And I'm Daniella. I'm a vegan. Aunt Sasha made a pumpkin cheesecake for me."

"No kidding? I'm a vegan, too."

Daniella beamed at him. "Are you staying for dinner? There's enough to share."

He looked over at Sasha's mom.

Valentina nodded, tears glistening in her eyes. "Please, stay."

Connelly came in from the den and draped

his arm over Sasha's shoulder. "Feeling thankful?"

She nodded. But her heart was too full to speak. She wondered if Matthew liked rock climbing.

THANK YOU!

Sasha and Leo will be back in their next adventure soon. If you enjoyed this book, I'd love it if you'd help introduce others to the series.

Share it. Please lend your copy to a friend.

Review it. Consider posting a short review to help other readers decide whether they might enjoy it.

Connect with me. Stop by my Facebook page at www.facebook.com/authormelissafmiller.com for book updates, cover reveals, pithy quotes about coffee, and general time-wasting.

Sign up. To be the first to know when I have a new release, sign up for my email newsletter at www.melissafmiller.com. Prefer text alerts? Text

BOOKS to 636-303-1088 to receive new release alerts and updates.

While I'm busy writing the next Sasha book, if you haven't read my Bodhi King, Aroostine Higgins, or my We Sisters Three series, you can pick up the first book in each of those series now:

AUTHOR'S NOTE

October 28, 2020

This book is set in 2019 rather than the present day for several reasons. In case you're a reader who cares about that level of detail, here are the primary reasons: One, COVID-19. I couldn't very well have Sasha running around unmasked in close contact with so many characters during a pandemic; nor could I envision a book where she did all her investigating via Zoom call and spent the rest of her time washing her hands. Two, 2019 is the twentieth anniversary of Patrick McCandless' death, and that feels like the sort of significant milestone that would have a heavy impact on the family's day-to-day life. And three, I conceived of this plot before the deaths of George Floyd and Breonna Taylor and the subsequent Black Lives Matter protests this spring and summer garnered national attention. I couldn't see my way clear to have an officer-involved shooting in my fictional world that took place in the Fall of 2020 without addressing the real-world situation. So November 2019 it is. (At least in Sasha's world.)

For my research lovers, predictive policing is real. If you're interesting in learning more, here are some resources to get you started:

- Here's a great video explainer on pre-crime policing in Los Angeles: https://www.wired.com/video/watch/pre-crime-policing-how-cops-are-using-algorithms-to-predict-crimes
- A similar program is in place in Pasco, Florida: https://projects.tampabay.com/projects/2020/investigations/police-pasco-sheriff-targeted/intelligence-led-policing/
- This article describes a predictive artificial intelligence program that *was* (but is no longer) being

developed right in my backyard: https://www.wired.com/story/algorithm-predicts-criminality-based-face-sparks-furor/

- And Cesare Lombroso, the "father of criminology," was a real person: https://www.history.com/news/born-criminal-theory-criminology and https://en.wikipedia.org/wiki/Cesare_Lombroso

Finally, I wholeheartedly apologize for naming a character Jordan *and* a character Jordana. Jordan (Sasha's sister-in-law) first appears in *Irretrievably Broken*, and Jordana (Sasha's intern) makes her debut in the novella *A Mingled Yarn*. Both characters appear in multiple books, but not until now, when they appear in the *same* book, did I realize how confusingly close their names are.

On a similar note, we first learned that Sasha's brother was shot by his friend Cole in *Irreparable Harm* and that Cole is mentioned throughout this book. Astute readers will note that, in *Irrevocable Trust,* a boy who enters the Witness Protect Program also takes the name

Cole. The second Cole (who is adopted by Hank) appears in multiple books in this series.

I promise I don't do these things to confuse you. But, speaking of confusion, Sasha and I both have cats named Java—only her Java is a male cat, and mine is a female. You can only imagine how many times per book my editors have to change "she" to "he" when I am referencing that fictional feline!

P.S. Sasha isn't much of a baker, as you may know, but she did have success with these vegan pumpkin mini-cheesecakes. https://minimalist-baker.com/vegan-pumpkin-cheesecake/

ALSO BY MELISSA F. MILLER

Want to know when I release a new book?

Go to www.melissafmiller.com to sign up for my email newsletter.

Prefer text alerts? Text BOOKS to 636-303-1088 to receive new release alerts and updates.

International Incident

Imminent Peril

The Humble Salve (Novella)

Intentional Acts

In Absentia

Inevitable Discovery

Full Fathom Five (Novella)

The Aroostine Higgins Novels

Critical Vulnerability

Chilling Effect

Calculated Risk

Called Home

Crossfire Creek

Clingmans Dome

The Bodhi King Novels

Dark Path

Lonely Path

Hidden Path

Twisted Path

Cold Path

ABOUT THE AUTHOR

USA Today bestselling author Melissa F. Miller was born in Pittsburgh, Pennsylvania. Although life and love led her to Philadelphia, Baltimore, Washington, D.C., and, ultimately, South Central Pennsylvania, she secretly still considers Pittsburgh home.

In college, she majored in English literature with concentrations in creative writing poetry and medieval literature and was stunned, upon graduation, to learn that there's not exactly a job market for such a degree. After working as an editor for several years, she returned to school to earn a law degree. She was that annoying girl who loved class and always raised her hand. She practiced law for fifteen years, including a stint as a clerk for a federal judge, nearly a decade as an attorney at major international law firms, and several years running a two-person law firm with her lawyer husband.

Now, powered by coffee, she writes legal thrillers and homeschools her three children. When she's not writing, and sometimes when she is, Melissa travels around the country in an RV with her husband, her kids, and her dog and cat.

Connect with me:
www.melissafmiller.com

Made in United States
North Haven, CT
03 September 2023